Changeling Press, LLC
ChangelingPress.com

Obsession (Raven's Vale Psychos 1)
Contemporary Dark Fiction
Harley Wylde

Obsession (Raven's Vale Psychos 1)
Contemporary Dark Fiction
Harley Wylde

ISBN: 978-1-60521-798-7

Publisher:
Changeling Press LLC
315 N. Centre St.
Martinsburg, WV 25404
ChangelingPress.com

Printed in the U.S.A.

Editor: Crystal Esau
Cover Artist: Bryan Keller

The individual stories in this anthology have been previously released in E-Book format.

Table of Contents

Obsession (Raven's Vale Psychos 1)
Contemporary Dark Fiction
Harley Wylde

I'm a monster.
The Boogeyman.
The thing you fear in the dark.
I've killed countless men and women, and I have
no plans to stop.
They locked me up. Called me insane.
Until I escaped.

Raven's Vale is mine. Well, partially mine.
Crash and Kane help me rule over this small town.
I've never wanted anything other than watching
the life fade from someone's eyes after I've taken
my knives to them.
Until Hollis.

She makes me question whether there's still a
heart beating in my chest.
For some reason, I want her... and I don't want to
kill her.
I want her under me. Submitting to my every
whim.
But I crave her fear too.
She's my obsession...
And I'll stop at nothing to make her mine.

Prologue

Riot

Smoke filled the room as both Crash and Kane smoked like fucking chimneys. The shit bothered me, and they both damn well knew it. Not that either of them gave two fucks. They'd settled in for a game of cards, but the darkness outside called to me. My skin itched and my fingers twitched. How long had it been since I'd last killed?

Too long.

"What the fuck crawled up your ass?" Crash asked. "Isn't it almost your night? You should be pretty damn stoked."

"Not soon enough," I muttered. "Besides, being offered a lamb to slaughter isn't as much fun as hunting one."

Kane nodded. "I get it. They reek of fear either way, but it's always sweeter when they aren't expecting it."

"There's something seriously wrong with you two," Crash said. "I don't understand your fascination with getting all bloody. My way is much better. Nice and neat."

Kane snorted. "They still end up dead, don't they? Don't pretend you're any better than us."

Crash shrugged. It was an old argument. The three of us had stumbled across this town when Crash and I had barely been considered adults. Kane was a bit older than the two of us. Freshly escaped from an institute for the criminally insane, we'd needed a place to hide. Raven's Vale boasted a population of no more than five thousand. Cut off from the larger towns and cities, it had been the best place for us to lie low.

If it hadn't been for the fire we'd set, or the fact

we'd managed to keep them guessing over how many bodies had burned to death, the law would most likely have been searching for us all these years. Instead, they believed we were dead. Anywhere else, we'd need things like driver's licenses, birth certificates, or something to prove who we were. Not in Raven's Vale.

Then our cravings had kicked in. We hadn't been able to help ourselves. Not long after we started slaughtering anyone who crossed our path, we found ourselves face-to-face with the mayor and sheriff. It had been easy enough to convince them to bow to us. After the mayor received a few pieces of his daughter, and the sheriff realized we had his two girls as well, the tides had quickly turned in our favor. We'd released them back to their families once we knew the mayor and sheriff would toe the line. They both knew we could snatch them again at a moment's notice.

Now we ruled Raven's Vale. No matter how many we killed, no one was coming for us. None of them dared. And as far as the outside world went, none of them knew we existed. We didn't leave a paper trail.

"Get the hell out of here," Kane said. "You know you can't wait."

I flashed him a smile and flipped off Crash before I grabbed my knives and headed out. Eyeing my motorcycle, I bypassed it and decided I'd track down prey on foot tonight. The bike was fun to ride but noisy as fuck. Everyone would know I was coming long before I got there.

Although, sometimes it was fun to chase the rats when they started to scurry. Tonight wasn't one of those nights, though. Right now, I wanted to instill fear before they even realized who was stalking them in the shadows.

Most people feared the night and stayed indoors as much as possible. No one knew when one of us might strike.

Movement caught my eye, and I crept closer, clinging to the shadows. A young woman hurried down the sidewalk, her head bowed and shoulders hunched. If she was trying to make herself invisible, she'd failed miserably. I kept pace with her but remained out of sight. Something about her seemed different from the others in this place.

There was no way she didn't sense my presence. At some point, even the most dense individuals would realize a monster was stalking them. If she did, the woman never let on. She continued to wherever she was going.

For once, I didn't experience the urge to snuff out her life. Instead, I wondered what made her entirely oblivious. Was it a self-defense mechanism? She disappeared into an apartment building, and I figured that meant she was home for the night.

Going back the way I'd come, I walked the streets, hoping to find interesting prey. Two punks were doing their best to break into a car. The fact they didn't have permission to do this sort of shit in my town pissed me off. Rushing toward them, I ended one of their lives quickly with a slice across his neck. The other dropped his tools and backed up several steps.

"Holy shit!" He stared at his friend with wide eyes. "What the fuck?"

"That's what I'd like to ask." I prowled closer. "Who gave you permission to break into cars in this town?"

"Huh? What are you…" He paled. "Shit. Fuck! You're one of them, aren't you? One of the Raven's Vale Psychos."

I grinned. "Is that what everyone calls us?"

He tried backing up again and tripped over his own feet. The moment he landed on his ass, he pissed himself. Crouching in front of him, I held the knife where he could see his friend's blood coating my blade.

"Don't kill me," he pleaded. "This was all Rob's idea. I didn't want to do it."

"Uh-huh. Sure." Before he had a chance to move, I stabbed his thigh with my knife. The little pissant screamed and I stabbed the other leg.

He crab-walked backward, trying to get away. No point. He couldn't exactly run. Even if he did, I'd find him. Standing, I reached down and grabbed his collar, then dragged him along behind me. Down a dark alley, across another street, and into yet another alley. Dropping him by a dumpster, I took my time, sliding my knife into his belly, his legs, slashed his arms.

I could see the light fading from his eyes, and I sat to watch, taking it all in until he'd taken his last breath.

It didn't leave me feeling as satisfied as I'd hoped. Deciding there wouldn't be any others, I went back to the apartment building and watched the windows, hoping to spot the woman from earlier. I found her on the third floor, staring out into the night. She'd changed her clothes, and her nightgown molded to her curves. Even from here, I could see the peaks of her nipples through the material.

My cock hardened and I wanted to feel her under me. Chained to my bed, begging for mercy. The thought of her crying, hearing her pleas for me to set her free, was enough to make me smile.

I didn't know who she was, but I wanted to find

out.

She was the first in over a decade to make me want something other than death.

Chapter One

Hollis

Raven's Vale reeked of fear and blood. Happiness ceased to exist here, and escape was a dream for most. Survival consumed me daily, draining my energy.

"Morning, Hollis," Dr. Nora Fields greeted, her voice strained as I passed her clinic.

"Morning, Doc," I muttered, scanning the distance for the psychopaths that haunted our lives.

"Fresh bread!" Lyla shouted from the bakery doorway, her enthusiasm tainted by impending danger. "Get it while it's hot!"

"Thanks, Lyla," I said, buying a loaf and feeling my stomach growl in response. Hunger was just another problem in this town.

"Take care, Hollis," Lyla said. I noticed the way her eyes darted from right to left, as if scanning the area for danger. I knew why. Everyone in town did. The murderers' presence lingered like a dark cloud. Their monthly killing spree loomed over us.

"Will do," I replied with a forced smile. As I continued my errands, the air grew heavy with tension.

There they were: three menacing silhouettes casting shadows across the ground -- our collective nightmares materialized before me.

"Riot," I whispered under my breath, captivated by his imposing figure. He was the worst of them, the one who made even the other two psychos look like amateur hour. My pulse quickened as I watched him walk, his movements fluid and predatory -- like a fucking big cat on the prowl. Was it just me or did it seem like he was coming closer to me?

"Keep moving, Hollis," I whispered to myself, shaking off the strange mix of terror and fascination that gripped me. No good could come from staring at The Butcher himself. I had heard stories of what he'd done to those unlucky enough to catch his attention. And yet... there was something about him that made it impossible to look away.

"Fuck," I muttered, forcing myself to focus on my errands, trying to push the image of Riot from my mind. I couldn't let my curiosity get the better of me -- not in this town, and certainly not with him. But damn if it wasn't hard to forget that face -- the face of the devil himself. Why did he have to be so sinfully gorgeous?

My heart hammered in my chest as I turned a corner, trying to distance myself from the chilling sight of the psychopaths. The wind howled like a banshee through the darkened streets of Raven's Vale, carrying whispers of terror and pain. I tried to shake off the unease that tightened around me like a vise.

Get your shit together, Crane. I knew if I didn't, I'd be next on their list. The town was holding its breath, waiting for the next blood-curdling scream or gruesome discovery to shatter the fragile illusion of safety. We were all just playing our parts in this fucked-up game, and it seemed I had drawn the short straw today.

"Hey, Hollis!" a voice called out, causing me to jump. I turned to see my friend Lyla hurrying toward me, her eyes wide with concern. "You okay? You look like you just saw a ghost."

"Something like that," I admitted, glancing over my shoulder one last time. The psychos seemed to have disappeared, but I couldn't shake the feeling that I was being watched. *Fuck*! I realized my suspicions were right. My gaze locked on to the piercing eyes of Riot Tredway. He was watching me -- not just watching but studying me. His eyes held an intensity that sent shivers down my spine and made my pulse race. "Riot."

"Riot?" Lyla asked, following my gaze. She gasped, pulling me behind a nearby building. "What the fuck is he doing here?"

"Watching us, apparently," I replied, my heart pounding like a jackhammer. "We need to get out of here."

I could feel Riot's gaze burning into me. It made me feel stripped bare and completely vulnerable.

"Come on," I whispered to Lyla, trying to drag her away from our hiding spot. "We need to move."

But try as I might, my legs refused to listen. They were rooted in place, paralyzed with fear. And it wasn't just fear -- there was something else too. I couldn't deny the perverse fascination I felt, the sick curiosity that drew me to him like a moth to a flame.

"What's wrong with me?"

"Nothing," Lyla reassured me, squeezing my arm. "It's just fear. Let's go."

"Right," I agreed, finally managing to tear my eyes away from his chilling stare. "Let's get the fuck out of here."

The looming presence of The Butcher cast a dark shadow over the streets, his name a whispered curse on the lips of those who dared not speak it aloud. Riot's gaze seemed to pierce through the veil of reality itself, drawing me closer with a magnetic pull that both terrified and intrigued. His eyes held secrets, hinting at a depth of darkness that sent a shiver down my spine.

Every step I took away from him felt like a battle against an invisible force, urging me to turn back and face the unknown. The air was heavy with unspoken danger, each heartbeat echoing like a drum of impending doom. As Lyla's whispers urged me to flee, I couldn't shake the feeling that this encounter was just the beginning of something far more sinister. The tangled web of fate seemed to weave tighter around us, entangling our fates with threads of uncertainty and dread.

But despite my terror, I saw a strange allure in Riot's gaze, a forbidden curiosity that beckoned me closer even as my instincts screamed to run. The promise of danger and mystery, tempting me toward the unknown depths of darkness that awaited.

In that fleeting moment of hesitation before our escape, I sensed a shift, as if destiny itself had taken hold of our lives. I walked with Lyla back to her bakery, leaving Riot's haunting gaze behind.

I did my best to stay away from Riot the rest of the day. As night fell, a chill skated down my spine. The streets of Raven's Vale were empty, the shadows creeping in closer as the sun sank below the horizon. I could feel eyes on me. The sensation was like a thousand tiny needles pricking at my skin. It was that fucker Riot Tredway -- I knew it. There had been times throughout the day it felt like someone was watching me. Since this morning, I hadn't spotted him again, but I'd known he was there.

Everywhere I looked, I saw nothing but dark corners and deserted alleys. But someone seemed to always be watching me. I could feel it. Didn't matter if I could see him or not.

"What do you want with me?" I called out, trying to sound braver than I felt. My voice echoed through the empty street, the sound bouncing back at me mockingly. No response came, but the oppressive weight of his presence remained.

"Damn it," I whispered, quickening my pace. My heart pounded in my chest, blood thundering in my ears. I couldn't let him see how much he affected me -- how much he terrified me.

I turned a corner, nearly colliding with a tall figure that seemed to materialize out of the darkness. I stumbled back, cursing, before realizing it was Riot himself.

"Watch where you're going," he said, his voice low and dangerous.

"Fuck off," I snapped, quickly regaining my footing. If he sensed weakness, it would only make things worse. I had no choice but to appear as strong as possible. I couldn't appear to be prey to him. If I did, I was done for.

"Feisty," he murmured, smirking down at me. "I like that."

"Get bent." I pushed past him and continued on my way. The brief interaction left me shaken and angry -- but most of all, vulnerable. It was like he'd reached inside me and grabbed hold of something, squeezing it tight until I could barely breathe.

The wind sliced through the air, carrying the smell of blood and decay. I shivered, pulling my jacket tighter around me as I hurried down the street.

I stopped at a rundown café, ordering a steaming cup of coffee to warm my chilled bones. As I sipped the bitter liquid, I saw him again, watching me from across the street. Riot's eyes bored into mine, his gaze predatory and unnerving. I felt a familiar unease coil in the pit of my stomach.

"Still following you, huh?" The barista, an older woman with sad eyes, shook her head. "You gotta watch yourself, Hollis. That man's got a taste for blood."

"I know," I admitted quietly, staring down into my now cold coffee. I couldn't deny the warped attraction I felt toward Riot, and it only seemed to grow stronger with each passing day, each brief encounter. I hated it, but something inside me craved it too.

"I need to get out of here."

"Be careful," the barista warned, her voice full of concern.

"Always am," I lied, forcing a weak smile before stepping out into the biting cold once more.

I didn't make it far before hearing Mayor Rawlins' voice boom out from behind me. "Hollis Crane!"

"Mayor? What's going on?" I asked, turning to face him.

"Riot… it's time for another sacrifice. One life to save hundreds. He's been watching you. We all know it. It has to be you, Hollis."

I knew the town offered up someone every month. It didn't seem to stop the killings, but they did seem to be slower than the months they didn't offer one. I understood the reason behind it, but it didn't mean I wanted it to be me!

"Me?" My heart pounded in my chest, my blood running cold. "Why?"

"Does it matter?" Mayor Rawlins snapped, anguish etched on his face. "I'm sorry, Hollis. There's nothing I can do. You know the rules we live by."

"Fuck you! You're just gonna hand me over to that monster?"

"What choice do we have?" he asked, desperation in his voice. "If we don't, he'll kill us all!"

"Then let him," I said. "I'd rather die fighting

than be some sick bastard's plaything!"

"Enough!" Mayor Rawlins roared. "You will be the next sacrifice, whether you like it or not. It's for the greater good."

"Fuck the greater good!" Deep down, I knew he was right. My life was nothing compared to the lives of everyone in Raven's Vale.

As I walked away, my thoughts turned one last time to Riot Tredway. He'd become an obsession, a dark force that haunted my every waking moment. And now, it seemed, he would be my downfall.

I hurried home, my heart pounding in my chest, my senses on high alert. I glanced up at the rooftops and into the darkened alleyways, but no one was there. I closed the door behind me, triple-checking the locks before collapsing onto my bed.

"Lunacy," I muttered, drawing my knees to my chin. "It's gotta be."

But even as the words left my lips, deep down, I knew it wasn't lunacy at all. The Butcher of Raven's Vale -- Riot Tredway -- had his sights set on me, and I didn't know why.

The wooden door splintered. The cold grip of a strong hand pulled me from the safety of my apartment and dragged me downstairs to the street. My vision blurred, but I could still make out the anguished faces of Dr. Nora Fields and Sheriff Dalton as they watched, helpless.

"Let her go, Goddamnit!" Nora shouted, her voice cracking with emotion.

"Back off, Doc," one of the thugs holding me snarled. "This ain't your fight."

"Like hell it isn't!" she insisted, but Dalton held her back, his eyes filled with silent apology.

"Please, don't do this," I whispered, my heart

pounding with terror.

"Shut up, bitch," the thug said, tightening his grip on my arm until I winced in pain. He and the three others worked for the mayor's office. Their sole job was making sure the sacrifices made it into Riot's hands. At least three times a year, Crash and Kane also accepted sacrifices, but they didn't slaughter as many people as Riot did.

"Leave her alone!" A new voice joined the fray, and I turned to see an older lady I'd spoken to a few times pushing through the crowd that had gathered. Her face was a mix of worry and determination, her fists clenched by her sides. What was her name? Right.

"Stay out of this, Mrs. Norris," I begged, not wanting her to get hurt on my account.

"To hell with that," she snapped, glaring at the man who gripped my arm. "You can't just take her!"

"Watch us," the thug sneered, shoving me toward another man waiting nearby.

As I stumbled, I caught a glimpse of Riot watching from the shadows. His piercing eyes were locked onto mine, and for a brief moment, something flickered behind them -- something other than bloodlust. But it vanished as quickly as it appeared, swallowed by darkness once more.

"Get her in the car," the thug ordered, his voice cold as ice.

"Please," I choked out, tears streaming down my face, "don't do this."

"Sorry, sweetheart," he replied with a cruel grin. "But it's you or the whole town."

"Fuck you!" Mrs. Norris retorted. "That sweet girl never hurt anyone."

"Stay out of it, hag," he growled.

"Take care of yourself, Mrs. Norris," I whispered

as they threw me into the car.

I glanced back and saw Lyla in the crowd. Out of everyone there, why hadn't she tried to stop them from taking me? Instead, she'd stood by, silently watching the entire thing. The car began to move, and the last thing I saw before we disappeared around a bend was Lyla's face, and what I'd have sworn was a smile.

My heart pounded like a drum in my chest. I clenched my fists, trying to steady myself against the fear that threatened to engulf me.

"Look who we got here," a thug sneered as they dragged me from the car and shoved me toward Riot. I wondered if they delivered the sacrifice to him in the same spot every time. "Your latest prize, Butcher."

"Leave her with me." Riot's voice was low and dangerous. The thugs exchanged glances before scurrying away, leaving me alone with the man who haunted my nightmares.

"Please," I whimpered, my knees trembling as I stared up at his imposing figure. "Don't kill me."

"Silence," he snapped, his eyes burning into mine. I flinched, feeling a wave of terror wash over me. My mind raced, desperate for any way to save myself from this monster. "Riot, I know there's more to you than what everyone sees. I've seen it in your eyes. You don't have to do this."

"You know nothing about me," he said, grabbing my arm and pulling me close. "I am a fucking killer. That's all you need to know."

"Then why haven't you killed me yet?" I shot back, defiance flaring up within me. "If you're really the monster they say you are, why am I still breathing? I've seen you following me. You could have slit my throat at any time."

"Maybe I'm just savoring the moment. Or

maybe, just maybe, there's something about you that intrigues me. But don't mistake that for mercy, girl. One wrong move, and your blood will paint these walls."

"Then I'll make sure not to give you a reason," I replied, my voice shaking but determined. "If you let me live, I'll show you there's more to life than death and bloodshed."

"Bold words," he mused, releasing my arm and stepping back. "But can you back them up?"

I swallowed hard, knowing that my life hung in the balance. "I can try."

"Good," Riot said, his expression unreadable. "You'd better pray you succeed, or this will be your final act of defiance."

As I stood there, trembling before the man who could end my life with a single swing of his blade, I knew everything had changed. Something had sparked between us, a connection neither of us fully understood.

And as I stared into the eyes of the notorious Butcher of Raven's Vale, I found myself filled not with terror, but with anticipation for what would come next.

Chapter Two

Riot

I stared at Hollis' trembling form, savoring the fear tainting the air around her. It was thick and heady like the scent of freshly spilled blood. I circled her, smiling as she trembled. Defenseless. And mine.

"Let's make this a bit more… interesting, shall we, little mouse?" I grabbed her by the arm and forced her to meet my gaze. "You have a choice, Hollis. You can either let me carve my art into your soft skin… or…"

She tensed, her eyes darkening as fear overtook her. I leaned in, breathing in her scent and flicking my tongue out to trace the line of her jaw.

"Or you can be a good girl and accept my hospitality."

"Wh-what… what do you want from me?" she asked.

I couldn't help but laugh at her naïvety. "I want to see you squirm, dollface. To watch as you drown in the filth and depravity that lies just below your pretty surface. So, what'll it be? My knife or my… company?"

I could practically see her thoughts scroll across her face as she contemplated her options. Tears slipped down her cheeks, and I knew she'd made her choice. "Fine. I-I'll… I'll… accept your… hospitality."

"Good girl." I dragged her into the mansion I shared with Crash and Kane. Up the stairs and down the hall to my room. Slamming the door shut behind us, I stared at her in anticipation. "Now, strip."

She seemed paralyzed with fear at first, then slowly began to obey. Once she stood completely bare, I let my gaze trace over every inch of her curves. My cock became rock hard behind my zipper, and I couldn't wait to make her mine.

I trailed my hand down her spine and over her hip. Fear rolled off her as I unbuckled my belt and slid down the zipper on my jeans. "Beg me."

She shook her head, and I heard a whimper escape her. Looked like my little mouse wasn't going to play nicely. But she was new to this, so I'd make an allowance or two.

"Beg me," I repeated.

"Please… don't hurt me."

"Say it," I demanded.

"S-screw you," she said.

I grabbed her by the hair, yanking her head back so our eyes met. "Careful, pet. I can make this feel a whole lot worse."

Defeated, she muttered, "Fine. Use me. Just… Don't hurt me."

I couldn't help but laugh a little. No one had ever defied me the way she did. Not and lived to talk about it. And yet, here she stood, still unblemished.

"Your spirit won't do you any favors. It only makes me want to beat it out of you."

I dragged her, naked and trembling, over to my bed. The door opened, and I cursed as I glanced over at Crash and Kane.

"Did you bring a toy home?" Crash asked. "Last time you killed your sacrifice in the streets. But it looks like you want to play with this one a little more."

"Get the fuck out," I said, turning back to Hollis.

I heard the door shut, and knew they'd listened. For now, anyway.

"You won't find mercy here, Hollis. Not from the likes of us." I secured handcuffs around her wrists, shackling her to my bed. "So tell me. Are you a virgin? Will I be the first one to fuck your tight little pussy?"

Her face flushed and she looked away. I forced her to keep her gaze on me. The way she didn't want to answer told me plenty.

"You've been touched by others?" Jealousy ripped through me, and a red haze settled over my vision. I wanted them. They needed to pay for touching what was mine. "Tell me, Hollis, who else has had the pleasure of defiling you?"

Hollis gasped for breath, her face flushed with humiliation. "N-no one. I-I swear, it was just my toy... and... and a few times... I-I mean, I was desperate, all right? I had no choice!"

My grip on her throat tightened. "Clarify 'I had no choice.'"

Hollis' eyes watered as I released her throat and pressed my forearm against it, applying more pressure. "A few men. I was desperate and needed money. They paid me to suck them off."

I could barely contain my rage as I hauled my hand back and slapped her across the face. Red bloomed on her cheek and tears leaked from her eyes. "No fucking excuses! Who? Where?"

Her resolve seemed to crumble. "Alleys, public bathrooms. I sucked them off and they paid me because I was starving, okay?"

"I asked who, Hollis."

"Randy Gilbert, Matt Hayes, and Rusty West. Are you satisfied now?"

"I'm going to fuck you, Hollis. And when I'm done, you'll know what it means to belong to me."

I stood and stripped out of my clothes. She paled as she watched me, and yet, I noticed a flicker of heat in her eyes. She might say she didn't want this, might even fear me to some extent, but she couldn't deny she wanted me. I stroked my cock as I looked down at her.

"Spread your legs," I said. Her cheeks turned even redder as she obeyed me. "That's it. Show me that pretty pussy."

I worked on my cock until I came all over her, my cum covering her lower belly and dripping between her thighs. Putting my dick away, I fastened my pants and leaned down over Hollis.

"I'm going to go take care of a few things and I'll be back. Be a good girl and don't cause trouble. You won't like it if Crash and Kane come in here while I'm gone. Understood?"

She nodded and remained silent.

I stormed out of the house and hit the streets, searching for the vermin who had dared to touch her. One by one, I hunted them down.

Randy Gilbert was easy enough. I found him balls-deep in a whore, fucking her against a building. Walking up behind him, I slit his throat, the blood spraying the whore's face. She screamed and as his body fell to the pavement, she didn't even bother lowering her dress before she took off running.

Rusty West was next. I kicked the drunk fucker's leg, trying to get his attention from where he'd sprawled outside the liquor store. He blinked up at me and saluted with a mostly empty bottle of cheap booze.

"You had the audacity to touch what wasn't yours," I said.

"Whatcha talkin' 'bout?" he asked, his words slurring.

"Hollis Crane. You put your filthy dick inside her. Now I have to cut it off." At my words, he paled and began to sputter as he tried to get away. Drunk off his ass, it wasn't like he was getting anywhere fast.

Yanking him to his feet, I dragged him into the closest alley and shoved him against the side of the building. Using my knife, I sliced open his pants, and snarled at the pathetic lump of meat hanging between his legs. With one quick move, I hacked it off, letting it flop to the ground at our feet.

He screamed and squealed as blood gushed down his thighs. "That's for touching what didn't belong to you."

I stood back, watching as he slumped to the ground. It took a while, but the light began to fade in his eyes. Soon, death claimed him.

Two down. One to go.

Matt Hayes was harder to find. Snug in his bed at home. I typically didn't barge into people's houses. I left them with the false sense of security the four walls gave them. In this case, I'd make an exception.

I broke the knob and entered the house, marveling at the fact the bastard hadn't bothered to lock a deadbolt or even put a chain across the door. He was making this far too easy. Creeping through his home, I found him in bed, with either his wife or girlfriend. I pressed the blade of my knife to his neck.

"Time to pay for your crimes, Matt Hayes," I said.

The woman gasped and sat up in bed, staring at me in terror. Matt was a little slower to rouse, and when he finally spied me leaning over him, he gave a shout and tried to scramble away. For the sheer amusement of it, I let him go, nearly laughing as he threw the woman my way.

"Don't kill me," she pleaded.

"I'm not here for you. I'm only here for him," I said, following after Matt. Once I caught up to him, I made quick work of ending his miserable life. I sliced his wrists, his femoral artery, and then cut his throat. I left him dying on his kitchen floor and left as quietly as

I'd arrived.

One last stop before returning home. I couldn't very well be jealous of a piece of machinery Hollis had used to get herself off, but it didn't mean I couldn't find a use for it. Getting into her apartment was easy since someone had broken down her door.

Everything remained as she'd left it. Not a thing out of place except some dirty clothes. I rifled through her bedroom, dumping her dresser drawers on the floor. Pausing a moment, I realized she'd have no clothes to wear except what she'd had on earlier. I picked up a handful of things and shoved them into a duffle I found in her closet. The nightgown I'd seen her in before, a few pairs of panties and bras, three pairs of jeans, and a modest selection of shirts. It wasn't like I planned to let her leave my room anytime soon. Perhaps one day I'd trust her enough to let her loose. But only after I knew for certain she'd come right back.

I didn't know what was so different about Hollis. Never in my life had I ever wanted to keep someone. It wasn't like she was a pet, and I'd never had one. I didn't get attached to people or things. There might have been a time when I was a child I'd tried to hold onto things, but it had been so long ago I didn't remember it very clearly. I'd done my best to wipe my childhood from my mind. The only things I'd kept since then were my journals, mostly because I didn't want anyone getting their hands on all my inner thoughts and my exact number of kills.

Finally finding the toy in her bedside table drawer, I tossed it into the bag as well, and the bottle of lube sitting beside it, then made my way back to the mansion.

* * *

Hollis cowered against the headboard, her eyes

wide with fear. I liked that. Fear. Respect. I demanded it all.

"They're gone now. Only you and me left."

She didn't reply, merely stared at me. I held up the toy, "And as for this, I'll think of a use for it."

Her cheeks flushed a shade of crimson that I swore even the shadows couldn't hide. "I... it's not what you think. I haven't had it very long."

"Long enough. Did you bleed when you used it?" I asked.

She nodded slowly. Christ! She'd popped her own damn cherry with a hunk of plastic.

"Mouth. Pussy. Both already used." I leaned into her space. "Then I guess that leaves your virgin ass."

She gasped but seemed to be frozen in shock. Or perhaps something else. Heat bloomed across her cheeks, making her face even redder, and her eyes darkened. Her tongue flicked out to lick her lips, and I knew I'd turned her on with my words.

My cock pulsed with need, and I wasn't sure how patient I could be. I'd enjoyed the screams and pleas of my victims for decades. Even when I'd been arrested, I'd never confessed to all my crimes. If I had, they'd have known I started killing people when I was only eight. My first victim had been a woman who'd decided to crawl into my sleeping bag one night. I had no idea where my father had been. Possibly fucking one of the moms on the trip. That one kill had opened a door that had been firmly shut until then. Once I'd started, I didn't want to stop.

I'd run and she'd chased after me. Little did she realize I'd had a knife on me. Once we were far enough away no one would hear her scream, I'd sliced the bitch. Not once. Not twice. I'd hacked at her until she was unrecognizable.

By the time her body had been found weeks later, animals had eaten most of her. No one had ever been able to trace her disappearance to me, and they never would.

"You're scared of me, aren't you, Hollis?" I asked.

"Y-yes."

"Good girl. Keep being truthful with me. Even though you're scared, you feel something else too, right?"

She slowly nodded. I stared at her breasts, smiling as the nipples hardened under my gaze.

Reaching down, I pinched one of the hard nubs between my fingers, giving it a twist. She cried out, her body bucking. I gave it a sharp tug, making her scream in pain. There it was. That's what I needed.

I quickly stripped out of my clothes and joined her on the bed. Using the lube I'd swiped from her apartment, I coated two fingers and slid them inside her pussy, pumping them in and out. She thrashed under me, her body tensing. Drawing her knees up, she tried to escape my grasp.

"Uh-uh. I don't think so. You agreed to give yourself to me in exchange for not dying. Remember?" I twisted my fingers and drove them into her deeper. "That means every inch of you is now mine. Don't worry, Hollis. You'll soon be begging me to fuck you."

She shook her head, but her body betrayed her. I felt her pussy grip me tighter, then the heat of her release. Easing my fingers from her body, I lubed the toy and slid it in. A flat section fit over her clit, and I turned the vibrations on high.

Tears slipped down her cheeks as she came again, her body twisting and contorting, as if it were too much for her to handle. Settling over her, I used my body to keep her still. After her fourth orgasm, she started to plead with me.

"Please, Riot. I can't… I can't take any more."

"You'll take whatever I give you and ask for more. Understood?"

She nodded and gazed up at me. Her eyes looked so beautiful, and I leaned down to kiss her. I'd never wanted to taste a woman's lips before. My tongue slipped into her mouth, and I fought the urge to devour her. She whimpered softly, and her body became pliant under me.

Using the lube, I slicked my finger again and toyed with the tight hole between her ass cheeks. She tensed for a moment, until another orgasm hit, and it relaxed her enough I was able to slide my finger inside her. I worked it in and out, before adding a second one.

I'd thrived on pain for so long, but hearing her cry out in pleasure was even more enticing. My cock had pre-cum leaking from the tip as I leaned back and sat on my knees. Lifting her legs over my arms, I spread her open. The toy continued to buzz on her clit and inside her, driving her crazy. With a gentle push, I worked my dick inside her ass, nearly biting off my tongue as I struggled to maintain control of myself.

Once she'd taken all of me, I knew I couldn't hold back any longer. Driving into her with long, deep thrusts, I took what I needed. I fucked her until sweat slicked our skin, and she'd come twice more. The next time her ass clenched down on my cock, I pumped load after load of cum into her.

"Next time, I'm filling your pussy," I said, reaching down to turn off the toy. I eased it from her body before pulling my cock out of her. Heading into the bathroom, I washed the toy and myself. When I returned to Hollis, she'd fallen asleep, hands cuffed over her head.

I locked the bedroom door and released the cuffs. Massaging her wrists, I noticed they were already starting to bruise. I eased her over to the side of the bed and refastened the cuffs, putting her in a more comfortable position. Then I curled my body around hers and shut my eyes.

It was my first time sleeping with a woman in my bed, but oddly enough, I didn't mind it so much.

Chapter Three

Hollis

I woke with a jolt, my heart pounding. My wrists were still cuffed to the damn bed, the cold metal biting into my skin. Panic surged through me like ice-cold water, and I thrashed against my restraints, desperate to escape. But it was no use, I was trapped. Just like a damn fly in a spider's web.

The room was dimly lit, an amber glow seeping in through the curtains. Despite the lavish room, a monster inhabited it. Riot Tredway, The Butcher himself. I'd heard the stories, but nothing could prepare me for the beast who'd claimed me last night.

As I wriggled under the covers, I winced at the aches and twinges I felt. I should have been terrified, ready to run. But as I lay here, a part of me trembled not with fear, but anticipation. What was wrong with me? The man was utterly depraved! I should be loath to have him touch me, and yet, I felt a heat building inside of me at the mere thought of having his hands on me.

My breath caught in my throat as a tall, dark figure loomed at the foot of the bed. It was him. Riot. His eyes were as cold as the grave, boring into mine, and I swore I could feel his gaze all the way to my very soul.

"Morning, Hollis," he said, his voice deep and menacing. "Had a rough night?"

My mouth went dry, and bile rose in my throat. "Let me go, Riot. If you aren't going to kill me, then release me."

He chuckled, and the sound chilled me to the bone. "I don't think so, Hollis. No, I don't think so at all. You see, I have plans for you."

Plans? What the fuck did he mean by that? Fear clawed at my insides, but I refused to show weakness. "You're no different than the rest of the monsters in Raven's Vale."

He was on me in an instant, his hand around my throat, squeezing just enough to make me gasp for air. "Oh, Hollis," he whispered, "I'm not just any monster. I am *the* monster. The one your mama warned you about."

His grip tightened, and my vision started to swim.

"I hope... you... rot in hell," I managed to rasp out.

"We have some unfinished business."

With each passing moment, I felt his fingers clench more around my neck, choking me just a little more. The fear coursed through my veins, and yet there was something else mixed in with it -- an odd sense of arousal. He knelt down before me, his face barely an inch from mine, and I saw the madness in his eyes.

"What do you want from me?" I managed to whisper between ragged breaths.

He leaned in closer, his hot breath caressing my neck. "Your heart," he growled softly. "I want your beating, quivering heart in my hands."

I didn't understand how I could feel both terrified and turned on, I felt a strange sort of excitement at his words. His dominant presence was intoxicating, and it awakened something deep inside me -- a desire to submit, to be his completely.

As he leaned in farther, his lips brushing against my earlobe, I found myself melting under his touch. His hand traveled down my body, stopping just above my thigh. He nudged me gently toward him, and I complied without thought.

Our bodies were pressed tightly together, and I could feel every inch of his hardness against my aching pussy. I moaned softly as he began to grind against me, eliciting a shiver of pleasure from deep within. His other hand moved up to cup my breast.

"You are so beautiful," he whispered in my ear, his voice rough with desire. "So fucking perfect. So... *mine*."

I arched my back instinctively, pushing my breast farther into his hand. My thoughts were spinning, my body on fire. I couldn't believe how much I wanted him, how much I needed him to take control. It was as though he had cast some sort of spell over me, and I was powerless to resist.

"Say it," he commanded.

"Please," I whispered back. "Take me."

With that, he pulled me closer still, his lips finding mine in a searing kiss that left us both breathless. His tongue dove deep into my mouth, tasting and exploring every inch as his hands roamed freely over my body.

I knew I should pull away, at least try to escape him. This was wrong on so many levels. I'd been sacrificed to this man, and he'd used me. So why did I feel like I was burning from the inside out? Why did I yearn for his touch now that I'd experienced it once before? I felt like I was losing my mind.

The kiss deepened, our tongues entwining as his fingers traced along the lines of my collarbone. His touch sent shivers down my spine, making me whimper into his mouth. I couldn't help but arch my back to grant him better access to my body, begging for more even though I knew this was wrong.

He pulled away from the kiss, his hot breath

fanning across my flushed cheeks. "You're so fucking beautiful," he growled, his eyes drinking in every inch of me. I felt myself blushing harder, unable to meet his gaze as he continued to explore every curve of my body with his hands.

His thumbs brushed against my sensitized nipples, causing me to gasp and squirm under his touch.

"I want you," he whispered against my skin, his voice rough and demanding. "I don't know why, but I feel like I'll go mad if I don't devour every inch of you. Bend you to my will. Brand my scent on your skin and make you mine in every way possible."

I tried to buck and toss him off me, but he was too strong for me. He pinned me against the bed with one hand while the other slid up the inside of my thigh, lightly brushing against my pussy. He growled again when he felt how wet I was for him, thrusting two fingers inside of me.

"Please," I moaned helplessly as he started to move in rhythm with those two fingers buried deep inside of me. It felt so good, so wrong yet so right at the same time. I wanted him to continue even though I knew I shouldn't.

He pulled his fingers out of me slowly, leaving a trail of wetness along my thigh as he lowered his hand. This time there was a wicked glint in his eye that sent shivers down my spine -- a prelude to whatever he had planned next for me.

Taking a deep breath, he leaned in and pressed his lips against my neck, claiming it as his own, sucking gently at the pulse point. It was both erotic and terrifying, sending shivers down my spine and making me tremble underneath him. He leaned back and unfastened his jeans, pulling out his cock. He stroked it slowly, and I stared in fascination. I hadn't gotten a good look before. Had that really been inside me?

He straddled my body, coming closer. His cock mere inches from my face. He guided it toward my lips, and painted my lips with his pre-cum. I saw the gleam in his eyes.

"Taste me," he demanded, and I found myself nodding weakly as he braced my head with one hand and pressed the tip of his cock to my lips. His scent enveloped me -- masculine and musky with an underlying hint of danger.

I parted my lips hesitantly and took just the tip into my mouth, savoring the taste of him. It was salty and warm, and made me shiver with need. He groaned deep in his throat, encouraging me to take more as he began to push farther inside. My eyes fluttered closed as I took him deeper into my mouth, letting myself give in to this forbidden pleasure that consumed every thought except for him.

His hips bucked against me urging me on while my clit started to pulse with need, and I pressed my thighs together, trying to ease the ache. He pulled out abruptly and eased down my body.

"You had the audacity to take your own innocence with a vibrator. Now you'll find out what it's like to be filled with cum." He leaned down, his lips near my ear. "I'm going to fuck every hole you have, until there's no doubt who you belong to. I'll come down your throat, in your pussy, and I'll fuck your ass. There's not one single inch of you that isn't mine. Do you understand?"

"Yes. I understand," I whispered.

"Good girl."

* * *

Lining my cock up with her pussy, I thrust into her hard and fast, filling her up. Tears leaked from the corners of her eyes as I used her, taking what I wanted. Her nipples were hard and erect, belying the fact she enjoyed what I did to her. When she looked at me, I could see the heat in her eyes, even if she didn't want to admit she desired me.

I pounded her pussy until I couldn't hold back. I felt my balls draw up and I pumped my cum into her, giving her everything I had. When I'd finished, she lay beneath me, limp and trying to catch her breath.

"What if I had a disease from those men?" she asked. "Did you ever consider that?"

I smirked at her. "What if I'm the one carrying something? Not that you have any business asking."

She shuddered and my smile widened. I knew I was clean. Until Hollis, I'd not fucked a woman in years. Sexual urges weren't something that bothered me. No, it was the whispers that came to me, telling me to spill blood. Those I would heed. Slicing up worthless pieces of flesh always made me hard, and there'd been a time I'd found a random woman and fucked her, willing or not. But this... having Hollis handcuffed to my bed, was the best I'd ever had.

I got up and went to the bathroom, starting the shower. I'd uncuff her long enough for the two of us to get cleaned up, and depending on how she behaved, I'd let her go downstairs with me. One wrong move, and she'd be right back on the bed.

I released her and carried her to the bathroom. Picking up one of my knives from the counter, I showed it to her. "Try to run, and I won't hesitate to stab you. Understand?"

She nodded quickly, her gaze locked on the blade. I trailed the tip of the knife along her collarbone. She trembled and I felt a spike of adrenaline. Sliding the blade down farther, I circled her nipple. The fear in her eyes was addictive, and I wanted more.

"Remember when I said I'd make you mine in all ways?" I asked. "I'm going to cut my name into your skin, then I'm going to fuck you again. And you're going to take it, aren't you?"

She whimpered but didn't pull away. Good, it meant she was learning. Perhaps one day, I'd be able to set her free without worrying she'd run off or hide from me.

Backing her into the shower and against the tiled wall, I pressed my body against her, pinning her in place. Gripping the knife in my hand, I didn't take my gaze off hers. The pain and fear fueled my desires as I etched my name into her hip. As I dragged the blade down to finish writing the T, she finally cried.

My beautiful Hollis sobbed as I turned her to face the wall. Grabbing her neck, I forced her to bend over, and I kicked her feet apart. Rubbing my cock along her pussy, I made sure to brush against her clit with every stroke. Soon, I had her whimpering for another reason.

"That's it. Tell me what you want, Hollis."

"You. I need… I want you."

"Beg me." I'd never wanted anyone as much as I craved her right now.

"P-please," she stuttered. "T-take me."

I took her. Claimed her. Shoving my cock into her pussy, I didn't go slow or easy. I dropped my knife and slid my hand through my bloody name on her hip before easing my palm around her to her belly. Reaching between her legs, I rubbed her little clit in hard, tight circles. She shattered, her cries of pleasure making something inside me break free. A beast I'd never known was hidden in me.

I leaned down, pressing my chest to her back, and bit into her shoulder, marking her with my teeth. She screamed as I broke the skin and the coppery taste of her blood hit my tongue. And still I kept fucking her.

I made her come twice more before I shot a load into her and pulled out. My cum slid down her thighs, mingling with the blood still oozing from my name on her hip. The water at our feet turned pink with a mixture of cum and blood, and I'd never felt more satisfied.

I quickly washed and watched as she did the same, smirking as she winced when the soap hit my name. It looked nice. Rough. Ragged.

"Get dressed." Without another word, I shut off the water and got out. I dried myself briskly and tossed her a towel.

She waved a hand to my name on her. "This is going to bleed through my clothes and stick to the fabric."

"You can use the stuff in the cabinet to treat it, but if it doesn't leave a scar, I'll be carving it again."

As I pulled on my jeans and a tee, I watched as she quickly doctored the wound and pulled on the clothes I'd brought from her place.

The way her hands shook, and she kept casting glances at the door, told me she feared leaving this room. Whether she thought I'd kill her, or she worried about Crash and Kane was a mystery. I held out my hand to her, and she took it, letting me lead her from the room and down the stairs.

Crash and Kane stared at her, their eyes narrowed. I knew what they were wondering. Why the hell hadn't I killed her? Because I found her much more fun alive than dead. My very own little toy.

"Well, well, well," Crash drawled, his voice dripping with poison. "Look who finally decided to join the party."

I glared at the asshole and flipped him off.

Kane snorted, his laughter devoid of mirth. "I knew it was only a matter of time."

How the fuck had he known I'd keep her? I hadn't even realized I was craving something like this until now. It bothered me, thinking he could see me clearer than I ever knew myself. Or was he talking about something else?

"You knew I'd keep her?" I asked.

He shook his head. "I meant you had to come down sooner or later. You aren't the type to hole up in your room with a woman for days. Unless you're torturing her."

"Leave us," I said. My brothers stood and left the room, but I saw the way Crash eyed Hollis, and I didn't like it. I had a feeling he'd cause trouble sooner or later.

It looked like Kane had cooked today. Bowls of eggs, biscuits, and bacon sat in the center of the table. I grabbed two clean plates and some forks, then motioned for Hollis to sit. She obeyed without question, and I filled a plate for her. We ate in silence, and I contemplated why I wanted more from her than death.

What made Hollis Crane so special?

Chapter Four

Hollis

The door creaked open, and Riot's hand brushed against the small of my back, urging me into a cluttered sanctuary. The stale air was thick with dust and secrets. Shelves sagged under the weight of old leather-bound books, their spines cracked and faded. In the dim light, I could see personal trinkets scattered like relics of a life I couldn't begin to understand. He pulled a chain, and a naked bulb flickered above, casting an unforgiving glare on the walls lined with what I assumed were his memories.

"Here," he grunted, pointing toward a stack of black journals, each one more worn than the last. "My thoughts, uncensored. If you've got the guts, take a peek."

I hesitated, but curiosity was a persistent itch, demanding to be scratched. My fingers trembled as I reached for the top journal, its cover cold and smooth. Flipping it open elicited a crack from the spine that echoed through the silence.

The words leapt off the page, sick and vile, recounting deeds that would make the devil himself wince. Each sentence was a blow, each paragraph a stab, painting scenes of brutality in ink. Yet, I couldn't stop, drawn in by the raw honesty of his savagery. It was repulsive, the way he detailed the infliction of pain with the precision of a surgeon and the glee of a child ripping wings off flies.

"Can't handle the truth of me?" Riot's voice sliced through the quiet.

His question hung unanswered as I turned another page, the horror unfolding before me like a car crash in slow motion -- impossible to look away from.

The descriptions cut deep, leaving marks no one could see but felt down to the bone. I realized then, amidst the gore and the madness, that Riot was more than a monster -- he was a man torn apart and stitched back together with barbed wire and broken glass.

"Keep reading," he dared, the challenge laced with something that might have been pride or maybe defiance. It was hard to tell with the shadows clinging to his face, turning his features into an unreadable mask.

So I read on, the lines blurring between disgust and fascination, the twisted words binding me to him one line at a time. Each page was a piece of Riot laid bare, and I couldn't help but wonder if beneath the bloodshed, there was someone worth saving -- or if I was just another victim caught in his web of insanity.

It was clear he'd started these while he'd been locked up. Everyone in town heard the story of where these men came from. It wasn't a big secret or anything. In fact, they'd used it to instill fear into all of us. I didn't know why he'd bothered to smuggle them out when he'd been on the run. But within the pages, I learned his secrets. The things he'd suffered as a child, the way he'd been treated while locked up, and all the nightmares he'd faced -- first by himself, and later with Crash and Kane by his side.

"Did these things really happen?" I asked, glancing up. He gave a short nod. "So your parents really…"

"Yes. They really did loan me out to their friends from the age of nine to be used however they saw fit. The man who hurt me the most was my second kill. Do you want to know why?"

Did I? I wasn't sure, but I waited to see what he'd say.

"The first woman wasn't intentional. She'd tried to crawl into my tent when I was eight years old. I'd lured her away from the campsite and killed her, then left her for the animals to feed on. But it showed me how much I enjoyed it, and I knew I could do the same to the others."

Others? I waited for him to continue, letting him speak and tell me as much as he wanted to. While part of me didn't want to hear it, I thought it might give me more insight into who Riot was and what made him tick.

"I fought the first time my dad's friend hurt me. Cried. Struggled. Did everything I could to stop it from happening. So my father held me down while the bastard shoved his cock into me. He raped me for what felt like forever." He crept closer, squatting beside me. "I waited until I knew he'd be alone, then I snuck into his house and slit his throat while he was sleeping. That was the moment I realized a quick death was too good for the likes of him. For all of them."

"And you went after the others next?" I asked.

He nodded. "They were all sadistic in their own ways. Perhaps I've always had darkness inside me. Maybe being used by those people only set it free a little sooner. Once I'd finished them off, it was my parents' turn. Since dear ol' dad had held me down the first time one of his friends had fucked me, I tied him up so I could start with his fingers and make the pain last. That way even in the afterlife, he wouldn't be able to use his hands for anything. I can only hope he's getting a taste of his own medicine down in hell."

Bile rose in my throat. How could parents do such a horrible thing to a small child? But if he'd started out killing those who'd hurt him the worst way possible, what had changed?

"I see you have more questions," he said. "Here. Read another one."

I read for a while. I didn't know how long. My neck started to ache from staring down at the pages. Snapping the fifth journal shut, I looked up at Riot, as he towered over me. I could feel his gaze burning into me.

"Spit it out," he commanded, his tone void of warmth.

My pulse hammered against my throat, each beat screaming for me to run. But there was nowhere to go. And part of me didn't want to escape -- not yet. "You're not just… not just the fiend they say you are."

"Is that sympathy I hear?" His words were a challenge, as if he dared me to feel such a thing for him.

"No." I shook my head, forcing steadiness into my tone. "Just an observation. You've been through hell, haven't you? Doesn't excuse your sins, but it paints a fucked-up picture, doesn't it?"

"Judgment's easy from a distance," he said, his voice dropping to a dangerous murmur, "But you're in the thick of my world now. Can't ignore the blood on the walls when you're the one splattered in it."

"Never planned to ignore it," I said. "But I see the cracks in your armor, Riot. I see the bastard child of pain who learned to bite before the world could swallow him whole. And I can't blame you for the things you did back then. No one could endure so much and remain sane."

Of course, that didn't explain why he enjoyed killing so much now. The people in this town hadn't done anything to him. He'd likely killed others before getting here. Had it thrilled him so much he couldn't stop? Or like he said, had there always been darkness inside him?

A cruel grin tore across his face. "There's no redemption here, Hollis. Just survival. And you're neck-deep in the quicksand with me."

"Guess we'll see who sinks first," I muttered. Now that I'd seen another side of him, I couldn't paint him as a killer. Sure, he'd taken lives and continued to do so, but at one point he'd probably been an innocent child. His parents and their friends had created the monster he'd become. At least, that's what I wanted to believe. If I held onto that thought, then it made him more human, and made it easier to swallow my attraction to him.

The world stilled as Riot's hand reached out, a shadow moving through the gloom. His fingertips grazed my cheek with an unexpected tenderness. I leaned into his touch without thought, drawn to the warmth that belied the coldness in his eyes -- a moth fluttering recklessly toward a flame.

"Didn't peg you for gentle," I murmured, my voice barely above a whisper.

"Life's full of fucked-up surprises," he replied.

His thumb traced the line of my jaw. The quiet was a living thing, wrapping around us. I realized then, with a jolt that rattled my bones, the man who could snap necks like twigs had found a way to cradle my face as if it were something precious. And damn me to hell, I wanted him to hold it -- to hold me -- just a second longer. What sort of person did that make me?

"Comfortable?" he asked, the word hanging heavy between us.

"Strangely, yes," I admitted.

"Good." The word sounded like it was a promise of chaos yet to come.

I should've been scared, should've been planning

my next move to survive. Instead, I found solace in the eye of the storm, in the heart of the beast who'd shown me a glimpse of his human side -- a side as scarred and battered as my own. Oh, I hadn't lived through the same horror as him, but I'd also been abandoned by those who should have protected me.

"Riot," I started, the name tasting like a sin on my lips.

"Shh," he cut me off, his finger pressed lightly against my lips. "Don't ruin it. Not yet."

For a heartbeat or two, we remained locked in that impossible moment -- two broken pieces fitting together in the midst of madness. It was a fucked-up version of peace, but it was ours, and I clung to it like a lifeline.

When I'd been told I would be the sacrifice, I'd expected to die a horrible, painful death. Instead, I'd discovered The Butcher wasn't as black and white as I'd always thought. Instead, I'd found another soul just surviving in the only way he knew how.

A bang outside the room jolted me, rupturing the silence. My pulse jumped. Riot tensed beside me, his warmth vanishing as if it had never been there at all. He was on his feet before I could blink, his hand clamping around mine with an iron grip.

"Come." He yanked me up and dragged me toward the door. The gentle man from moments ago was gone, replaced by The Butcher, his face a mask of cold fury.

We spilled into the corridor, the dim light throwing harsh shadows across the walls. Crash and Kane loomed like specters, their eyes boring into us with the sharpness of knives.

"What's this shit, Riot?" Crash demanded, his lip curled with disdain. "You playing house with your little pet? You don't even let me and Kane enter that fucking room."

Kane stood silent, but his glare cut deeper than any of Crash's barbs, suspicion written in every line of his towering frame.

"Got a problem?" Riot's voice was like ice.

"Since when do you keep them breathing this long?" Crash stepped closer. "Thought you were about the kill, not the thrill."

"Seems like you're losing your edge," Kane chimed in, his voice a low rumble, the threat behind it clear.

"Or maybe," Riot countered, his tone unyielding as stone, "I'm just choosing my cuts more carefully."

What did *that* mean? Was I still in danger of losing my life to him?

Their gazes locked in a silent battle, the unspoken violence hanging thick between them. I stood there, caught in the crossfire, knowing I was the spark to their gunpowder. Whatever came next, it was on me -- the girl who'd looked into the abyss and dared to reach out a hand to save the monster lurking inside.

Riot's laughter was dark and rich. "You two are pathetic. Why don't you go snatch up some prey of your own, if you think it's so damn easy to keep a woman alive?"

Crash's fists clenched, veins bulging like ropes under his skin. "We aren't amateurs, Riot. We know the game. It's you who seems to have forgotten the rules. No attachments."

"Sometimes rules change," Riot said. "So the game continues, even if it's not quite the same as before. Are you scared you can't measure up? Or is it something else that frightens you?"

Kane's jaw tightened. "This little sideshow of yours better not be softening you up. Not once have you ever brought a woman here. You've always killed them before they could make it to the house. Something is clearly different, and I don't like it."

I could barely breathe, my heart hammering against my ribs. Their words were razor blades tossed carelessly in the air, and I stood in the middle, praying not to get cut. It was clear now -- my existence had tilted their world off its axis. What would happen to me if they decided to retaliate? I didn't think they'd go for Riot. Not right off. No, I'd be his weakness, and they'd do their best to destroy me.

"Enough!" Riot roared. "She's mine to deal with, not yours. And she sure the fuck isn't leaving until I say otherwise."

I realized then, standing among monsters, that I had become the linchpin of madness in Raven's Vale, the key to a door that should have stayed shut. What would happen when it burst open? Would I be the debris or the flame? And what the hell did it mean for the townspeople?

"Your pet project here," Kane said, voice low and lethal, "it changes things, Riot. Changes everything."

"Let it change," Riot said. "I'm the Butcher here. Not you, not Crash. Me. They may fear all of us, but you damn well know I'm the one who makes them all sleep with one eye open."

The air crackled with the energy of their hatred, a perverse triangle with me at the center. I was the anomaly. The wild card. And as they circled each other like rabid beasts, I couldn't help but wonder what my presence meant for the future of this hell we called home.

I'd thought getting closer to Riot would

guarantee my safety. It hadn't occurred to me how much Crash and Kane would resent my presence here.

Crash's fist flew at Riot. It connected with a sickening smack against Riot's jaw, the force of the blow snapping his head to the side. For a moment, silence hung heavy. Then Riot snarled, a feral sound that chilled my blood. He lunged forward, retaliating with a vicious hook that crunched into Crash's ribs.

I cursed under my breath, backing up against the cold wall as they traded blows. The thud of flesh against flesh was a drumbeat of impending doom, each hit echoing in the tight space. I braced myself, ready to dash out of the way.

"Enough!" Kane's voice cut through the chaos. He threw his weight between them, shoving them apart with arms that seemed made of steel. "Crash, go cool your damn head. Take a walk. Go swim. Something!"

Crash spat blood, hissing like a cornered animal, but he backed off. Kane turned to Riot, his tone dropping to a menacing growl.

"And you," he said, jabbing a finger into Riot's chest. "Don't think for one second that we'll sit back and watch you play house. Crash won't accept it, and neither will I. She's going to bring ruin to us all, and you fucking know it."

Riot's lips curled in a silent snarl, but he didn't move. Kane gave him a long, hard look before pivoting on his heel and stalking away. At times like this, I couldn't tell which of them was the leader. I'd thought it was Riot.

As Kane's footsteps faded, panic clawed at my throat. Would Riot turn on me now? Kill me just to keep the twisted peace he had with Crash and Kane?

"Riot," I whispered. "What happens now?"

"Quiet," he snapped, not looking at me. His knuckles were bloody, his breathing ragged.

I searched his face for any sign of what he might do, my mind racing. Could I make him see that I was more than a pawn in their sick game? That I could be worth fighting for? Desperation laced through me, binding my will to survive.

Whatever it takes, I'll make him see me as worthy of keeping. I knew if he lost interest, then I was doomed. I'd be lost to the chaos of the Raven's Vale psychos -- another grave and nothing more. And I'd do anything to keep that from happening, even fall in love with a monster.

Chapter Five

Riot

I snapped awake, darkness still permeating the room. The sheets tangled around me, and I kicked them off. My heart pounded against my ribs with every inhale, every exhale. In that liminal space between sleep and consciousness, two faces warred for dominion in my mind: Crash's sneering countenance, Kane's implacable stare.

Torn between friendship and… something else. Crash and Kane had been my family for more than a decade. But then there was her -- Hollis. She stirred something in me, something dormant and dangerous. Until Hollis, all I'd needed was the thrill of the hunt, the tang of blood in the air. I'd gotten off on watching the life fade from the eyes of the men and women I slaughtered. Now I wanted something more.

"Damnit," I muttered to myself. I sat up on the edge of the bed, my muscles tense and ready for whatever may come. Didn't matter that I was inside the mansion, a place no one would dare enter without our permission. Some behaviors could never be unlearned.

Her breathing was steady, rhythmic. Hollis. My captive. My… what? Not a victim. Never just a victim. She was a challenge, a puzzle box with a heart inside, beating just for me. Or so I told myself during those moments when the craving surged through my veins like wildfire.

I prowled over to where she lay, restrained. Her eyes fluttered open, wide and wary like a deer caught in the hunter's sights.

"Morning, dollface," I said, relishing the fear that danced across her features. "Sleep well?"

"Riot," she said softly. My name on her lips was a curse and a prayer all at once. I could tell she might hate me, but she also wanted me.

"Shh." I bent close enough for her to feel the threat of me, the heat rolling off my skin. "Don't speak unless you're spoken to."

She recoiled slightly, but something in her gaze held steady. Brave little bird. I could crush her, yet she dared to meet my gaze head-on.

"Remember who keeps you alive." I traced a line down her cheek, almost tender if not for the clawing need to dominate that thrummed through me. "Who your world belongs to."

"You," she said, the single word a tangle of resignation and something that didn't belong in the cage I'd built for her.

"Good girl," I praised with a smirk. "Don't forget it."

I studied her, the way she looked at me -- not just with fear, but with an unsettling curiosity. She was my enigma, wrapped in chains of my own making, yet somehow holding a key I couldn't quite see. I wasn't sure who I would be once I'd finished with Hollis. In my gut, I knew she was going to change me, even if I didn't realize how just yet.

"Today's going to be fun," I promised. "For me, at least."

And with that, I left her to stew in the room that was her prison -- and mine.

I returned to Hollis with a leather restraint in hand. I moved her to the bed, fastening the cuffs around her wrists again. She looked… beautiful. The mix of fear and anticipation in her eyes made me eager for what would come next. "You're not going to like this."

"Please, Riot… Don't hurt me."

"Shut up," I snapped, my tone sharp and unforgiving. My hands were steady as I checked the shackles around her wrists.

"Is this necessary?" she whispered, her eyes searching mine for an ounce of mercy.

"Everything I do is necessary," I said. For a moment, I allowed myself to brush my fingers against her arm, almost a caress, before I recoiled, disgusted with the weakness that surged within me. When it came to Hollis, I felt conflicted.

"Please… don't," she pleaded.

"Can't help it, doll," I said. "This is who I am."

"Who you think you have to be," she corrected. "There's more to you than this, and you know it, Riot."

"Silence!" I barked, my hand involuntarily flexing into a fist. Her bravery was a thorn in my side, and my desire to break her mingled with an infuriating urge to protect her.

"Riot, you can be more. You *are* more."

"Enough! You know nothing about me. You think reading a few journals means you know everything? You don't know shit!"

"Then show me. I want to know who you are. The real you."

"Be careful what you wish for," I warned, my voice low and threatening. The weight of my body pressed her into the mattress as I secured her ankles with leather straps, the finality of her captivity sending a rush of power through my veins. "You might just get it."

She went still beneath me, her chest rising and falling with rapid breaths. In that instant, something unspoken passed between us.

I stood back, observing my handiwork. My heart

thrummed with a sick satisfaction, yet the echo of her words haunted me. *Then show me.* What a cruel joke -- the monster and the maiden, caught in a battle neither of us might survive.

"Get some rest," I said, my voice a cruel mimicry of tenderness. "You'll need it."

With those final words hanging between us, I turned on my heel and left her alone, confined and vulnerable. Each step away felt like tearing flesh from bone -- agonizing, yet impossible to stop.

I stormed out of the mansion and sought to silence the monsters whispering in my mind. It didn't take long for me to find someone who'd dared to wander into a darkened alley. Walking up behind the woman, I sank my blade into her side. She cried out, falling to the ground. Rolling to her back, she stared at me, eyes filled with terror.

"Please! Don't kill me," she pleaded.

I felt... nothing. Why did I want to spare Hollis, but not this woman? My gaze scanned her body, and I didn't feel so much as a twinge of attraction for her. Kneeling over her, I pinned her wrists over her head with one hand, while I sliced the skin of her breasts, belly, and arms with my knife. After I'd made her a bloody mess, I slit her throat, and let her bleed out.

I prowled the streets a little longer but didn't find another victim. Returning to the mansion, I went straight to my room, and Hollis.

I sat on the edge of my bed, the darkness clinging to me like a second skin. Could Hollis peer into my soul, see the maelstrom within, and not flinch? The thought gnawed at my insides, a hunger for something more than fear in her eyes.

Can you really understand what I am? My hands clenched, the memory of her warmth under my grip still fresh. *Could you accept this... beast?*

A laugh ripped from my lips, bitter and sharp. Acceptance was a fairy tale, and I was no prince. No, there wasn't a point in asking my questions. I no doubt wouldn't like her answer, and then I might actually kill her.

The bed creaked as I leaned toward her, a predator closing in. She lay there, restrained, yet defiance sparked in her gaze. It was intoxicating -- a challenge.

"Comfortable?" I asked, looming over her.

"Go to hell," she said, glancing away.

I grabbed her chin, forcing her to meet my eyes. "You're already there, sweetheart. Might as well embrace the darkness. It's all you're going to know from now until the day you die."

Hollis tried to jerk away, but I was an immovable force. "I decide when you sleep, when you eat, if you scream."

"Riot --" she began, a plea lurking beneath her bravado.

"Shut up." I cut her off, my tone leaving no room for argument. I tightened my hold, relishing the power that surged through me. This was my world, and she was just living in it -- by my rules.

"Remember this. You are mine to command."

"I hate you."

"Good," I replied, a sadistic smirk playing on my lips. The hatred was easier to take than the possibility of something deeper.

Releasing her, I stepped back, watching the resolve in her eyes war with the fear. It was a dance I knew well, one that kept me on the razor's edge between man and monster. Not the fear, but desire... Usually it was a thirst for blood, but with Hollis, I wanted more. Fear was something I only recognized by looking into the eyes of my victims. Since I'd been a child, locked in a horror show of my parents' making, I'd never allowed myself to feel that emotion again. I'd carved it out of my soul with my first kill. But as I turned to leave, the smallest crack in my armor appeared, a sliver of doubt that maybe, just maybe, she could see the human behind the horror.

The room stank of fear and sweat. Her eyes, wide as saucers, followed every one of my movements. I could feel the beast within licking its chops, eager for the game.

"Let's see how much you can take."

"Riot, please." She whimpered, only fueling my need to dominate, to control.

"Silence." I gripped my knife. A different one than I'd used to kill the other woman. I traced the blade along her skin. A lover's caress entwined with terror. I pressed just enough to make her flinch, to let her feel the bite without drawing blood -- yet.

"Does it scare you?" I asked, my tone deceptively soft, watching her struggle against the restraints. "Knowing I can cut you open anytime I want? Strip the skin from your bones. Tear out your still beating heart."

She nodded, tears pooling in those damned eyes that saw too much. I hated that they made me pause, made me question. Made me… *want*.

Inside, a war raged. Every second with her, the lines blurred -- the killer and the man. Merging. Conflicting. I couldn't afford to be soft, not in this world, not when it could mean death. Crash and Kane were right to worry. If they thought for one second that Hollis had changed me, they'd either kill her, or do their best to end me.

"Then remember this fear," I demanded, letting the knife hover over her heart. "It's what keeps you alive."

But as I watched her chest rise and fall with panicked breaths, a gnawing ache filled me. A whisper that maybe, just maybe, there was more to this than the rush of power, more than the satisfaction of her submission. Although it was certainly delicious.

I pulled the knife away, and I stepped back, a predator robbed of his kill by his own confusing desires. When it came to her, I might enjoy the terror in her eyes, but I didn't want to slaughter her like I did so many others. No, I found it much more thrilling to fill her with my cock and make her beg for something other than death.

"Remember who owns you, Hollis." I despised the emotions swirling within me. Emotions had no place in my world, no place where brutality ruled supreme. But there she was, a crack in my armor.

Stripping out of my clothes, I covered her body with mine. She didn't tense or pull away. In her eyes, I saw nothing but acceptance.

She was mine, and I intended to take her in every way possible.

I reached down and roughly fondled her breast, pinching the hardened nipple between my fingers. She whimpered, her pupils dilating with desire. She was mine to torment and pleasure. I ground my hips against her, making sure she could feel how much I wanted her.

My mouth crushed against hers, fingers tangled in her hair as I forced my tongue deep into her mouth. She moaned, her body arching up to meet mine. I slid my hand down her stomach, tracing the contours of her ribcage before dipping between her legs. She was wet, soaking with need.

I pushed my finger inside her, filling her slowly, watching as she squirmed underneath me.

"Tell me how much you want this," I demanded, my voice husky with lust.

"I want you to fuck me hard," she panted, her breath hot against my ear. I pulled my finger free and pushed my thick cock against her wet pussy, feeling the heat of her body surrounding me.

"Do you remember your place, Hollis?" I asked, my voice low and menacing. She shook her head, eyes wide with fear and need. I thrust into her, hard and rough.

"Say my name," I ordered, pulling her hair sharply. She cried out, arching her back as I pounded into her.

"Please... Riot..." She trembled, and I let out a growl of approval, grabbing her throat and thrusting even deeper.

"That's better." I began to move faster, slamming into her over and over again, feeling her tight walls clench around me. "Fuck, you feel so good."

I groaned and leaned down to bite into her shoulder. She whimpered, pulling on the cuffs that bound her wrists above her head.

"Don't stop," she begged, her voice hoarse with desire. I had complete control over her body and mind. No matter what I did to her, she still wanted me.

With one final thrust, I emptied myself inside her, groaning as I felt her walls pulsate around me and I filled her with cum. I collapsed on top of her, panting heavily as we both caught our breath.

"That," I whispered, leaning in to nip at her neck, "was a reminder you belong to me."

"Riot?" she said softly, a question in her eyes that

probed at the raw edges of my soul.

"Stop looking at me like that."

"Like what?" she asked.

"Like I'm more than this. I'm not going to give you flowers. Take you out on dates. Give you some fantasy happy ever after."

"Maybe you are more." Her fingers flexed and I could tell she wanted to reach for me. If she touched me right now, I wasn't sure what would happen.

"Enough! Remember your place," I snarled, every muscle coiled tight.

"Riot --" she started, but I cut her off with a glare that could freeze hell over.

"Don't say my name like it means something to you," I warned, steel lacing my words.

"Understood," she whispered, her defiance bleeding out, and leaving vulnerability in its wake.

"Good." I got off the bed and took a step back, my eyes never leaving hers. Setting her free, I pointed to the bathroom, allowing her to relieve herself. Once she came back, I secured her again. She hadn't earned the right to roam free.

"Tomorrow, we start again. I can't trust you to roam freely in this room until I'm certain you know you're mine."

With one last look, I turned on my heel and strode to the door.

I didn't look back. I never did.

The door shut with a definitive click, echoing through the silent house. I stood outside, chest heaving slightly, the rush of exerting power still coursing through my veins. But it was always followed by the quiet, by the whispers of doubt that crept in like fog.

She was strong. Stronger than she had any right to be under my grip. Every time I left her, every time I turned my back, I felt it -- the pull, the Goddamn connection that shouldn't have been there. Was she getting under my skin? Or was I finally seeing myself in someone else's eyes?

"Fuck," I cursed under my breath, shaking off the thoughts.

But they clung to me, persistent as shadows at dusk. I stalked down the hallway, needing to put some distance between us.

The air felt heavier. My thoughts were a battleground, a war between what I wanted and what I needed to do.

I stopped dead in my tracks, slamming my fist into the wall beside me. The plaster cracked under the impact, a spiderweb of destruction that mirrored the fractures in my composure.

Get it together. You're letting a woman get under your skin.

She was supposed to be nothing more than a pawn, a plaything to amuse me until I killed her like all the others. But when she looked at me, those eyes didn't just see the blood on my hands -- they saw through the red, into the blackened heart I wasn't sure I possessed anymore.

A laugh, dark and humorless, scraped its way out of my throat. What a fucking joke. Me, Riot Tredway, "The Butcher" of Raven's Vale, caught in a snare of his own making -- with threads as fine as her hair and as strong as her spirit.

"Tomorrow everything changes," I muttered to myself.

With that, I walked away, needing as much distance between us as possible.

Chapter Six

Hollis

There were days when time passed slowly, and other times it flew by. Thanks to the TV in the room, I was able to at least keep up with the dates. The day of the next sacrifice loomed like a dark cloud over Raven's Vale, casting a shadow over the whole damn town. I felt it in my bones, that icy dread creeping up my spine as the day inched closer. I didn't have to walk around town to know everyone was on edge, glancing over their shoulders, Killing Day breathing down our necks like an omen of doom.

I didn't sleep a wink the night before, just staring at the filthy ceiling above me, waiting for the inevitable moment Riot would arrive. I didn't even hear him come. He was so damn quiet for such a big bastard. One moment I was shivering in bed, and the next, Riot had his hands on me, dragging me out of the room. At least I'd been able to dress the last time he'd been in the room. Although, as possessive as he seemed to be of me, I didn't think he'd let anyone else see me naked.

"No! No, please!" It was no use. He had me, and there wasn't a damn thing I could do about it.

Riot was silent as the grave, save for his harsh breathing, as he hauled me into town. My heart was about to beat its way out of my chest, my mind a frenzy of terror-fueled thoughts. *Is this it? Is this finally the end of the line for me?*

We stumbled down the darkened alley, garbage and God knows what else squishing under our feet. My stomach churned, and I swallowed back bile, focusing on anything but the bloody end I was sure awaited me. Had I not played by his rules? I didn't know what was happening, or why.

Riot shoved me against a damp brick wall, and my breath caught in my throat. Was this the end of the line? My eyes were wide, as I watched Riot reach for one of his blades.

"Please," I whimpered, "I'll do anything. Anything you want. Just don't --"

Riot's cold, dark eyes met mine and there was a flicker of... something. Confusion? Interest? I couldn't tell, and it wasn't the time to decipher the psychopath's thoughts.

Suddenly, with a swift motion, Riot turned and glanced down the alley. I saw the mayor waiting with another woman. He shoved the poor thing into the alley and Riot left me long enough to grab her.

Dragging her closer, he slammed her against the wall beside me. With his gaze locked on mine, he held out his hand. I didn't have a choice but to place my palm against his. He tugged me closer, placing me in front of him, facing the other woman.

She cried, but I saw the look of resignation in her eyes. Riot put the knife in my hand, and I nearly dropped it.

"Time to show me you can live in the dark with me, Hollis," he said. "Because if you can't, then maybe she can."

I sucked in a breath as his meaning hit me. He wanted *me* to kill her? And if I didn't, then he'd make her the same offer? What the hell?

"Riot, I..."

He wrapped his hand around mine, pressing my fingers tighter into the hilt of the knife. "It goes in just like you're slicing butter. Easy as can be. Come on, Hollis. Show me you have what it takes to be mine."

He nuzzled the side of my neck and I swallowed hard. Closing my eyes, I thrust the knife forward and felt it sink into the woman. She screamed out in pain, and I quickly released the handle and backed farther into Riot.

"Not a bad start," he said. He moved me to the side, but where he could keep me within sight.

With his gaze locked on mine, Riot stuck the blade into her stomach. Not once. Not twice, but three times. As she gasped and sputtered, trying to cling to life, he dragged the knife across her throat. Blood sprayed the opposite wall, and my screams mingled with the poor girl's gurgles.

The Butcher, the monster of Raven's Vale, had just spared me.

I slid to the ground, trembling in shock as Riot wiped his blade on the dead girl's shirt. I didn't understand. Why did I have to be the one to stab her first? What if I hadn't? Would he really have killed me and taken her home instead? He'd said I was the only one to make him curious about something other than murder. Now I had to wonder if it had been a lie.

He prowled closer to me, caging me against the wall with his massive body. Leaning down, his lips crushed mine in a dominating kiss. I had no choice but to surrender to him.

When he stopped, he dragged me from the alley and back to the mansion. We didn't slow until we'd entered his room once more.

My breathing was ragged, and my heart raced as I watched him grab a dirty shirt from the floor. With one menacing glance, he wiped the bloody knife on it before throwing it onto a pile of other weapons.

"Do you know why I spared you?" he asked, his voice low and dangerous. "You have the prettiest fucking body I've ever seen. And you're mine. The only woman to ever interest me in something other than killing."

My heart thumped against my chest as he towered over me, his gaze burning into my soul. I couldn't speak. All I could do was nod in agreement.

He grinned wickedly. "Good girl."

He dragged me by the hair and pulled me closer to him. Our bodies were pressed tightly against each other, and I could feel the heat emanating from him.

Without warning, he slammed me against the wall, pinning me there with his massive frame. His free hand reached down to grope my ass cheek, squeezing it roughly through my clothes. I gasped at his sudden roughness but couldn't help the wave of arousal that washed over me.

His lips met mine again, this time even more forceful than before. His tongue plunged deep into my mouth, claiming it as his own while he pushed his hips forward, grinding his hard length against my soaked pussy.

"Please," I moaned into his mouth, arching my back to get closer to him. "Fuck me, Riot."

He pulled away slightly, looking down at me with dark lustful eyes. "Not yet."

He ran a callused finger down my cheek.

I felt his rough hands on my hips, pushing my skirt up and exposing my bare ass. Riot groaned in approval as he spanked it, leaving a burning heat on my skin.

"I let you live, and now you're going to pay me… with your body." His hot breath tickled my ear. He quickly stripped out of his clothes, then picked up the knife again. He cut my clothes from my body, and I stared at the remnants, wondering if I'd have anything left to wear if he kept doing that.

He took my hand and led me over to the bed,

pushing me down onto it. His body hovered above mine, his hard cock pressing against my stomach. He trailed his fingers across my sensitive skin, tracing random patterns that sent shivers down my spine. He brushed his fingers over his name, where he'd etched it into my skin. He hadn't gone deep enough to leave a dark scar, and the way I saw him eye it the other day made me think he might cut it a little deeper before too long.

"You know you want this," he whispered huskily. "You want me to claim you as mine."

I bit my lip, too aroused to resist him. "Do whatever you want with me."

He smiled wickedly. His eyes filled with lust. "That's my girl."

He spread my legs wide, leaving me exposed and vulnerable beneath him. Before I could even process what was happening, he pulled me into a scorching hot kiss that left me breathless. His rough hands explored every inch of my body, leaving behind a trail of goosebumps in their wake.

It should have bothered me that he'd just murdered someone. Yet all I could think of was the way he made me feel.

I felt his warm mouth close around my nipple, sucking hard, and all other thoughts fled from my mind.

"You like that, don't you?" he asked, his voice low and menacing. I nodded frantically, unable to form words. He chuckled darkly and moved to my other breast, teasing it with his tongue before taking the nipple between his teeth and biting down hard.

I cried out in mixed pain and pleasure. He grinned wolfishly and moved down toward my pussy, teasing me with his hot breath.

"You're so fucking wet for me. I think you get off on being with a monster like me."

Without warning, he plunged his tongue inside me, licking and sucking on my swollen clit while his fingers explored my tight, wet pussy. I could feel myself starting to come, waves of pleasure washing over me.

"Fuck, yes! I need you inside me, Riot!"

He pulled away with a smirk, his eyes full of mischief. "Not yet."

He ran his hands through my hair. He then positioned himself between my legs and slowly pushed his cock inside me, stretching me as he went deeper and deeper.

I moaned loudly, feeling him fill me up completely. "Oh God."

I gasped as he began to thrust into me with a steady rhythm. It felt so good, so wrong, but I couldn't help myself. I wrapped my legs around his waist and held on tight as he took me harder and faster.

"You're mine. My little toy. My whore."

His hands found my still throbbing ass cheek, and he squeezed roughly. I cried out in pain as he continued to fuck me, his cock slamming into me over and over again.

We moved together in a primal dance of lust and domination, our bodies entwined in a display of raw passion. And as I felt another climax building inside me, I knew that I would never be the same again.

He groaned loudly, pushing himself deeper inside me as he came, filling me with his hot cum. We collapsed onto the bed, panting heavily as our heartbeats slowly returned to normal.

I looked up at him, feeling a strange mix of emotions: shame, excitement, and above all, a desire for more.

"Was it good for you?" he asked with a wicked grin. "Did you enjoy getting fucked by a killer?"

"It was…" I trailed off, unable to find the words to describe what we had just done. But I knew one thing for sure: I was addicted to this feeling of being taken, of being owned.

He grinned, his eyes dark and unfathomable. "Good. Because there's more where that came from."

Oh, God. If he didn't kill me with his knives, he might kill me with sex. Why didn't that sound like an awful idea? I wasn't sure how much more I could take, but he wasn't going to give me a choice. I both loved it and hated it.

"I will take you whenever I want. However I want." He reached out to grab a handful of my hair and gave it a tug. "And you're going to be my good little toy and do exactly as I say. Your life literally depends on it. You piss me off, try to run off, or break my rules, and it's game over."

The fear should have been there. The self-preservation kicking in to tell me to get out while I still fucking could. Instead, all I felt was anticipation. Anticipation for my new life as his plaything.

"Yes, Riot." I gasped, biting my lip as his grip on my hair tightened. "I'm yours. I'll be a good girl. I promise."

He smirked and released me. "Good."

As I stood up, his muscular arms flexed as he reached out to pull me closer. His touch sent shivers of anticipation down my spine.

"I want you to know that this is your choice," he stated, his voice low and velvety with a hint of roughness. "You can shower with me or face the consequences."

The way he eyed the bed I knew what he meant. I'd be handcuffed again and stuck in the bed. As I looked into his piercing eyes, all I could think about was how much I craved him inside me once again.

"I'll shower with you," I whispered back, already feeling the warmth spread between my legs. I felt like such a slut. Not once had I ever been interested in sex with a man. Not until Riot. Of all men for me to be insanely attracted to, why did it have to be a psychopath like him?

He led me into the bathroom and started the shower, then shoved me under the spray. He joined me and pulled me against his chest. His large hands roamed up and down my back slowly at first before gripping firmly just below my shoulder blades, pulling me into him even more forcefully while his tongue delved deep into my mouth exploring every inch hungrily.

He backed me to the tiled wall and pinned me against it while continuing to ravage my mouth. One hand snaked down to my ass and squeezed my cheek, while the other gripped my hair tightly.

"Riot, I need you."

"You are so fucking sexy when you beg for it like that," he said. He leaned in closer, causing goose bumps on my skin.

Without further warning or prompting, he slid two fingers deep inside of me stretching me wide before filling me completely. His touch sent waves of pleasure washing over every inch of my body.

He rubbed his cock against my belly. "Fuck! You feel so good!"

Lifting me, he forced my legs around his waist and slid his cock in deep. For some reason, his touch felt almost tender, even though he still took what he wanted. I felt the heat of his release inside me, and whimpered when he pulled out.

Riot turned me to face the wall and forced me to bend over. His hand cracked against my ass, and I yelped, feeling the sting. He spanked me again. And again. Each blow came harder than the one before, and my ass felt like it was on fire. I worried he might bruise me.

"Stop, please! What did I do wrong?" I asked.

He pressed against me, his cock wedging between my ass cheeks. "Not a damn thing. But I need you to equate pleasure with pain, Hollis. One day, you'll beg me for both. And that's when you'll be perfect."

I shivered, both fearful and turned on by his words. What was he doing to me? And why didn't I want to escape from him? Something was wrong with me. Maybe I was just as broken as he was, but in a different way.

"What am I to you, Riot?" I asked.

"I've already told you. You're my toy. Which means I can play with you however I want. Put my dick in all your holes. Spank your pretty ass. Wrap my hand around your throat." He bent over my back, placing his lips near my ear. "I could kill someone, make you watch, then fuck you right then and there. And there's not one damn thing you could do about it. Do you know why?"

"Because I belong to you?" I asked.

"That's right, Hollis. You're mine."

I shivered as he drew back and thrust his cock into me again. By the time he'd fucked me several times, my pussy ached, and I was so tired I could barely stay awake. I felt him carrying me to the bed, and the cool metal of a handcuff going around one wrist. Then the heat of his body behind me.

Riot was determined to drag me into his hell, and I wasn't sure I could do anything but go willingly.

Chapter Seven

Hollis

Just as Riot had promised, I was free. Sort of. At least, he'd no longer force me to remain tied to the bed, only freeing me for short breaks to use the bathroom or go down to eat with him. Sometimes he'd bring food up to me.

Now, I could at least move around. It seemed stabbing that poor woman had proven something to him, even if it had still taken him a little time to trust me this much. I still couldn't believe I'd done something like that. It felt like I had blood coating my hands, and every time I closed my eyes, I could still see her face. I didn't know if it was something I'd ever be able to get past.

The lingering question of *will he make me do it again* haunted me even more. Was it right for me to help kill someone else just so I could survive? What made my life more important than theirs? But at the same time, I wasn't ready to die. Not to mention, as much as I hated myself for it, I actually felt drawn to Riot. He scared the shit out of me, and yet, when he touched me, I wanted more.

A floorboard creaked behind me. I whipped around, heartbeat slamming into overdrive. Lyla stood in the doorway, pale eyes darting around the room.

What the hell? I glanced into the hallway behind her, and I didn't see anyone else. Why was she here? How had she gotten past Crash, Kane, and Riot? For that matter, last time I'd checked, the door had been locked. Unless Lyla picked up new skills, I didn't think she could break into the room on her own.

A ball of dread started to build in my gut. I'd considered Lyla a friend, until she'd watched as they dragged me off to be sacrificed. In all the time I'd been here with Riot, no one had come for me. Not that I knew of anyway. So, why had she shown up out of the blue? My senses were screaming at me not to trust her.

"Lyla, how the hell did you get in here?"

Lyla wrung her hands, inching toward me. "Crash and Kane let me in."

Bullshit. If they could easily walk in here, then wouldn't they have already dragged me out by force? I knew they didn't want me here. They urged Riot to kill me every damn day. So far, he'd held them off, but I always worried what might happen to me during the times he wasn't here.

How screwed up was it that I felt safer with Riot than without him? Maybe I really was fucked up in the head. Who fell in love with a psychopath?

Oh shit. My body tensed. Love? Why had I even thought that? I didn't love him. Nope. No one could ever love a man like that. Right?

Lyla shifted, and shut the door, drawing my attention to her once more.

"You've been working with them this whole time?" I asked, not thinking of another possible way she'd be standing here right now. Only Crash and Kane could have made this happen. Riot certainly wouldn't have. If he'd allowed her to visit, he'd have dragged her here and tossed her on the floor, then demanded to be repaid for his kindness of letting me have a visitor.

"No!" She stumbled forward, grasping my arms. "Hollis, you have to believe me. I came here and bargained with them to protect you. To get you out of here!"

I shoved her away. Yeah, right. How gullible did she think I was? If she was going to save me, she'd have done it before now. No, something else was going on, even if I couldn't figure out what just yet. I knew Crash and Kane hated me, but did they want me out of here enough to work with Lyla? Wouldn't it only make Riot angry when he found out what happened?

"Protect me? By conspiring with those psychotic bastards? What could you possibly offer that they'd want?" If I kept her talking, maybe something would slip out unintentionally. As much as I wanted to trust her and our friendship, I couldn't. There had been times I'd seen a flash of something in her eyes over the years, and now I wondered if it hadn't been my imagination after all. Had Lyla truly been a friend to me? Or had I merely grabbed hold so I wouldn't be so lonely?

"I'm trying to gain their trust so I can get you out of Riot's grip!" Desperation etched lines in her pale face as she edged toward me again. I had to admit, she sounded convincing. Except, I knew Lyla could lie her ass off when needed. I'd witnessed it before. This could all be an act.

"How stupid do you think I am? The only thing you're trying to escape is facing the same fate as me. What? If you get in good with Crash and Kane, you think your life will be spared? Is that it?" *Come on, Lyla. Give me something. Tell me the damn truth*!

Lyla's face crumpled, tears spilling down her cheeks. Damn. She really was a good actress. "Hollis, please. I never meant to hurt you."

I lunged forward, fisting her hair and yanking her close. "If you'd wanted to save me, you wouldn't have stood by and stared as the mayor dragged me off to be sacrificed. The fact Riot wanted me for something else is the only reason I'm still alive. So spare me the tears. The fact you're here at all is suspicious."

The floorboards behind us creaked again. Heavy footsteps were approaching down the hall. Riot? Or perhaps one of the others? Either way, I didn't think it would be good if I were caught in here with Lyla.

We both froze. Oh God, no. If it was Riot and he found her in here, I wasn't sure what he'd do. Crash and Kane would likely use this as an excuse to turn Riot against me, claiming I was trying to escape. But if it was Riot… I never knew what to expect from him.

The door opened and Riot stepped inside, his gaze raking over us. A slow, sadistic smile crept across his face. "Well, isn't this cozy?"

Shit! Why the hell had Lyla bothered to come if she was only going to cause me more problems? Unless that was her end game all along. Had Crash and Kane promised to protect her? I released her and faced him, pulse pounding.

"Riot, I can explain." Except, I really couldn't.

"No need." He prowled farther into the room, cracking his knuckles. "I think I've figured it out."

Lyla shrank behind me. I squared my shoulders, swallowing hard. "There's nothing to figure out. Lyla was just leaving. I'm not sure why she even came here, or how. It's what I was asking her."

"Is that so?" His tone was deceptively light, at odds with the threat in his eyes. "Because from where I'm standing, it looks like the two of you were conspiring against me. Did you decide to run away? You wouldn't get very far, Hollis. I told you. You belong to me now."

Lyla stepped from behind me. "I came to warn Hollis. Crash and Kane, they're planning to…"

Riot's hand snaked out, clamping around her throat. She gasped, clawing at his wrist.

"Don't. Lie. To. Me."

Lyla whimpered and her feet kicked as he lifted her up off the floor. My nails bit into my palms. As much as I didn't trust her right now, I also didn't want to watch him kill her. "Riot, stop! I'll tell you the truth."

His gaze flicked to me, brows lifting in mocking invitation. My heart pounded against my ribs. But if I didn't say something, he might kill her.

I took a deep breath. It was time to put my life in Riot's hands.

"Lyla didn't come to warn me," I said steadily. "She came to help me escape."

Riot's eyes narrowed. "Is that so?"

I swallowed hard, glancing at Lyla. Her face had gone pale, eyes pleading. But I couldn't back down now.

"Yes," I said. "Crash and Kane want me dead. You know it as well as I do. Lyla was going to help me sneak out of the mansion so I could get away."

"And you believed her?" Riot scoffed.

"I..." My voice faltered at the accusation in his tone. "I didn't. Not really. I was trying to get her to leave. It seemed odd that she suddenly showed up here, or that she managed to get into this room."

"You can always trust me." Riot eased his grip on Lyla's throat, though he didn't release her. "I told you I'd keep you safe, didn't I? That you were mine?"

"You did," I whispered. "I'm sorry for hesitating when she came here. I wanted to believe she was really my friend and wanted to help."

"Hollis, don't!" Lyla's eyes were wide as she stared at me. "He's lying, he'll never let you go! Please, you have to --"

Her words cut off in a choked gasp as Riot's hand tightened again. "Quiet, or I'll rip out your lying tongue."

And I knew he would do it too. No, he might even make *me* do it. "Please don't hurt her."

Although, why I was begging on her behalf I wasn't sure. It wasn't like she'd tried to stop them from taking me. She hadn't tried to save me in all this time. It didn't make any sense for her to be here now. Deep down, I knew she had to be scheming something, and Crash and Kane must be in on it.

Riot's gaze slid to me, cold and calculating. "And why should I show mercy to this bitch?"

"Because..." I faltered, scrambling for the right words. "Because she means something to me. She was my only friend all these years."

The words were true, even if I did question her friendship and loyalty. Until the day I'd been sent as a sacrifice, I'd always thought Lyla was a good friend. One of Riot's brows lifted in a silent challenge. I took a deep breath and steeled myself. It was time to make a dangerous gamble.

"She's like a sister to me," I said quietly. "If you hurt her... it would hurt me too." I really, really didn't want to watch him kill her. For a long moment Riot just stared at me, his expression unreadable. Then slowly, he loosened his grip on Lyla's throat. She slumped against the wall, gasping for air.

"Well, isn't that interesting? Do you think she feels the same? How very sisterly of her to leave you with me all this time. You don't find it odd that she's here now?"

I did and I'd even just said as much, which meant Riot wasn't fully listening to me. I knew Crash and Kane wanted me gone. Had they bribed her to come here? To what end? Were they hoping Riot would catch us and kill us both? I hadn't considered that until just this moment, but it made the most sense.

I swallowed hard. "I don't know why she's here. I really don't. But if you let her go, I swear I'll stay with you. You won't need to tie me down or anything. I'll be here willingly… for as long as you want me."

Riot seemed to consider it for a moment before releasing her. He stepped back and opened the door.

Lyla bolted, pausing only long enough to glare at me over her shoulder. "You're making a mistake, Hollis. You don't know what you're getting into."

Oh, I had an idea. But Raven's Vale wasn't a quaint southern town. It hadn't been peaceful, not since the three psychos came and took charge. Every day, we all lived in fear. At least here, I had an idea of what was going on, and might actually survive this hellish place.

Riot shut the door once more and folded his arms, staring me down. I wasn't sure what he wanted me to say or do. I'd already promised I wouldn't run. What more did he want from me?

"What?" I asked, not able to take his silence another moment.

"You want freedom? Want my trust?" he asked.

"Yes. I'll do whatever you want." I swallowed hard, hoping I wouldn't regret those words, but something told me I would.

"Then tonight, you're going to prove to me just how loyal you are, Hollis." He came closer, placing his hands on my waist. "Until then, I'm sure we can find other ways to pass the time."

My stomach growled and my cheeks flushed. "Um. Could we possibly eat first?"

He took my hand and led me to the kitchen. I didn't see Crash or Kane anywhere, for which I was grateful. Riot pulled things from the fridge, and I moved a little closer. When I realized he was making sandwiches, I decided to help. We worked in silence together, and I had to admit we felt like a regular couple in that moment.

We ate at the table, but I kept an eye on the door. The last thing I wanted was for Crash or Kane, much less both, to surprise me by showing up suddenly. I wondered if I should voice my concerns to Riot.

"Crash and Kane don't want me here," I said. "I promised to stay with you, but what if…"

"What if?" he asked.

"You aren't here all the time. Sometimes I'm alone. Do you think they would kill me?" I asked.

He paused. "I guess it's possible. But if they take something of mine, they know I'll retaliate. I may consider them brothers. They've had my back for more than a decade. Doesn't mean I won't gut them if I think it's necessary."

Damn. Did that mean none of us were safe from Riot? Ever? I wasn't sure how I felt about it, but I did like knowing he would avenge me if they murdered me. At least that was something.

"What do you want me to do, Riot?" I asked.

"I want you to survive and keep your pretty little mouth shut," he said. "Don't fuck with Crash and Kane. If you hear them coming, hide if you need to."

I wanted to ask if he cared about me, but I was too scared of what his answer might be. If he was only amusing himself by keeping me alive, I wasn't sure I wanted to know. Besides, the parts I saw of him outside of killing, made me want to know more about him. And the more I knew, the closer I felt to him.

Yeah, whether I liked it or not, I was falling in love with a killer.

I could only hope my heart could handle it.

Chapter Eight

Hollis

The cold bit into my skin as we prowled the streets of Raven's Vale, the night cloaking us in its sinister embrace. Riot moved with a predatory grace beside me, each step measured. Deliberate. A silent promise of the havoc he could wreak.

"Enjoying our evening out, Hollis?" he murmured.

"Thrilled," I lied, the word coming out more breathless than I intended. The darkness wasn't just around us. It began to seep inside, making itself at home in the pit of my stomach. I had a really bad feeling about why we were out here. He hadn't outright said anything, except that I needed to prove myself.

We turned a corner, and the sight of Raven's Vale's desolation sharpened. Buildings were deteriorating, their windows shattered or boarded up. Then we reached an alley, dimly lit by a flickering streetlamp that fought a losing battle against the encroaching shadows.

Riot halted, his gaze locking onto something -- or someone -- huddled against the grimy brick wall. A figure, shivering, trying and failing to melt into the darkness.

"See that piece of shit?" Riot's whisper cut through the silence, his lips twisting into a cruel smile. "Scum like that... they think the dark can hide them. But it can't -- not from me."

"Who are they?" My voice was steady, but inside, it felt like I was caught in a maelstrom.

"Doesn't matter who they were." Riot's eyes flashed with a dangerous light. "It's about what they've done. Thief, liar, cheat. Name your sin. Most people in this fucked-up town have rolled in it like a pig in shit."

A strange surge of anticipation coursed through me as I watched him, the dark maestro ready to orchestrate another round of terror. It was wrong, all shades of fucked up, but I couldn't deny the pull, the allure of what might happen next.

"Ready to see how deep the rabbit hole goes, Hollis?" He didn't wait for an answer, certain of his power, confident in the sway he held over me.

In the darkest corners of my mind, I knew I was lost to him. Whatever he demanded, I'd do without question. Riot might not be the gentlest man, but he'd given me more than anyone ever had. He wanted me. Desired me and *only* me. When would I ever find that again? And part of me hoped that maybe I could help him find at least some of his humanity. Although, there were times I wasn't sure he had any left.

Riot's bulk shielded me from the pale glow of the streetlamp as he gestured with a hand. "Move quiet. You need to be precise. Killing isn't about strength, it's about being smart and stealthy."

I held his gaze, wondering if I had what it took to do this, to walk by his side. The last time I'd been terrified, and it still felt like something I'd never get over. Could I possibly do it again? Or would I lose some part of myself in the process?

He leaned down and whispered low. "Find your inner darkness, Hollis. Let yourself be free. No constraints from the law. Toss your morality out the window. None of it matters here in Raven's Vale. Especially not when you're with me."

I nodded, more to myself than to him, feeling the cold kiss of the night air against my flushed skin. I edged forward, inch by painstaking inch, the rough brickwork of the alley's wall scraping against my palms.

"Remember, the slightest sound and your prey will run," Riot continued, his words laced with encouragement. "You're the predator here, not them. Let that sink into your bones. You are the one in charge, and you'll take what you want."

My breaths came shallow and fast, every inhalation a shuddering gasp as I closed the distance between myself and the quivering figure before me. The scent of fear was ripe, mixing with the metallic tang of anticipation on my tongue. My fingers twitched. Was I actually excited about this?

"Good... good," Riot murmured, his presence lurking behind me like an extension of my own shadow -- or perhaps it was more accurate to say I was an extension of his. "Now, make them feel the terror they've dealt in spades. It's time, Hollis. Do it."

I sprang, aiming for the man. Riot's teachings, his dark whispers, fueled my every muscle. The victim before me remained unaware, an unsuspecting lamb to my wolf. Maybe I was more of a wolf pup being taught how to hunt.

I knocked him flat, and gripped his throat with my hands, choking him into submission. He tried to buck me off, but I clung to him, refusing to back down. If I failed, I wasn't sure how Riot would react.

My sexy psycho placed a knife in my hand, and I jabbed it into the man's side -- quick, no hesitation -- just like he said.

"Fuck, yes!" His approval washed over me like a perverse benediction.

A warped euphoria surged within me, dark and addictive. I was the predator this time. For so many years, I'd been prey. Not only to Riot, but to anyone stronger than me in Raven's Vale.

I could feel Riot watching my every move. A teacher observing his student. Blood rushed in my ears. It felt like the person I used to be was leaving me in a rush, just like the blood of the man I'd stabbed. I was Riot's creation now, a reflection of his own monstrous heart. Each move was deliberate as I slashed and stabbed the man again and again.

His blood spattered the walls and myself, coating my hands and bathing the knife in red.

"Beautiful," Riot murmured. I knew, with a clarity that shattered the final pieces of my old self, I had crossed into his world -- a place where love and murder were inseparable, and eternal.

I was no longer the Hollis Crane who trembled in the shadows. Now I was the creature Riot had unearthed from within the grave of my former self.

"Fucking perfect," Riot said. His eyes were alight with a fervor that only the sight of blood could invoke. He watched as I became the very monster he'd envisioned, his masterpiece wrought in flesh and fear.

"Let it out, Hollis. Unleash all the pain from your past," he urged.

I obeyed, my actions painting crimson strokes on the alley, my personal canvas. Each scream that tore from the man's throat fueled my desire for more.

"God, yes!" Riot laughed, dark and sinister. There was pride in his words, a vile satisfaction in turning me into… this, whatever I was now.

"Beautiful chaos," he murmured. He stood over us, a puppeteer, reveling in the scene he'd orchestrated with his depravity.

Life ebbed from the wretch under me, a final gurgle escaping his lips. I stood there, shaking like a leaf. Blood painted my skin, warm and slick, and it was as if I could feel it oozing into my pores and staining my very soul.

"Riot?" I sought him, needing him to anchor me. Now that it was over, and I saw the carnage, my knees felt weak, and uncertainty filled me.

He closed the distance between us, and his gaze seared into mine. Without warning, his arms caged me, pulling me tight against the hard planes of his body. His embrace was possessive, and I could feel the thrum of his pulse, as we bathed in the afterglow of violence.

"You're a fucking natural." His words were both a caress and a brand. Whatever I'd been before, now I was a murderer just like him. A killer who enjoyed the hunt and taking a life. I shivered, lost in the maelstrom of what I had become, of what we now were together.

I leaned into him, needing his comfort. We were two halves of a whole, bound by the screams we silenced.

"Let's get out of here," he said, his grip tightening for a moment before he released me, a silent command that I follow him back to our sanctuary -- a mansion as twisted as we were.

As we started to walk farther down the alley, his hand found mine, fingers entwining with an intimacy that was as terrifying as it was thrilling. Our steps echoed, a symphony of depravity that played to the night. And I knew then, with every fiber of my being, that there was no turning back from the abyss that yawned before me. Riot had shown me the darkness, and I had embraced it with open arms.

I clung to Riot, my nails digging into the taut muscles of his back. Tremors racked my body. His dark aura enveloped me, the heat from his skin igniting something feral inside. A line had been crossed, one I'd never be able to take back. I felt it like a jagged tear in my soul. Could I ever claw my way back to the person I was before? Did I even want to?

The cold brick of the alley wall scraped against my back as Riot pressed me to it, but I didn't care. His hands were on me, urgent, rough. His desire was raw, like an untamed beast sating its urges. He yanked my pants down around my knees, then turned me to face the brick. My cheek pressed against it, the blood of the dead man squishing under my skin.

With one deep thrust, Riot entered me, making me cry out in surprise and a flash of pain. He fucked me like a man possessed, not caring who might pass by, or the fact we were standing in blood. He was intense and savage as he took what he wanted.

"Riot!" His grip on me tightened.

"Mine! Only mine." His movements were relentless, each stroke deeper, claiming me in ways I never imagined could stir such dark delight within me.

"Yours," I breathed out, surrendering to the rhythm of his possession. It wasn't just my body he conquered but something deeper, a part of my soul I'd laid bare for him to ravage.

I wanted to reach down and touch my clit, but I didn't dare. I only got to come when he allowed it, and right now, he was all about dominating me. And I loved it.

"Harder," I urged, craving the punishing thrusts of his cock.

Riot complied, his pace unyielding, fervent as if each moment was both an end and a beginning. His breaths came out in harsh pants, echoing off the walls.

"Look at what you've become." His voice was laced with pride and something darker, more dangerous.

"Your masterpiece?" I asked between moans, the words cutting through the haze of pleasure-pain.

His laughter was a low rumble against my neck, sending shivers down my spine.

"Yes. My perfect little killer. My whore who craves my touch, even when I give her pain," he said.

I came so hard, I screamed out his name. He powered into me until I felt his cock swell and then the heat of his release as he came inside me. Riot pulled out and yanked my pants up. I turned to face him, clinging to him. It felt as if he'd branded me as his in every way possible. Now, I was his forever.

I glanced down and the victim's lifeless eyes bore into me, accusing and unforgiving.

Riot took my hand, his touch surprisingly gentle. We walked back toward the mansion, our steps in sync.

"Ready for more?" he asked, his lips curving into a sinister smile that promised untold horrors and ecstasies.

"As long as I'm with you, I don't care what we do." My voice was steady. Together we moved through Raven's Vale, the town that belonged to the monster beside me and his two brothers in chaos. The world he'd painted in shades of red, and now shared with me.

Riot opened the door, and it groaned on its hinges. I stepped inside with Riot right on my heels.

"Welcome home," he said.

Yes. Home. There was no turning back now. Maybe there had never been a chance of surviving any other way. My hands were as stained as his, my soul just as tainted.

The foyer's dim light flickered across his face, casting half of it in eerie shadow while the other half basked in a sinister glow. It was the perfect metaphor for the man himself -- a creature of duality, both guardian and destroyer.

"Feels right, doesn't it?" he murmured, closing the distance between us with predatory grace.

"Like I was always meant to be here," I admitted, my words raw with the truth of them.

A chuckle rumbled from his chest. "That's because you were, Hollis. You're one of us now."

His thumb trailed along the inside of my wrist, tracing the pulse that hammered there. I already wanted him again.

"Us," I echoed, the word branding itself upon my very being. In this place, bound to this man, I was reborn -- a monster just like him, forged in blood and bound by desire.

Riot lifted me into his arms and carried me to our room. He kicked the door shut behind us and went straight to the adjoining bath. He eased me down, and I started to strip off my clothes while he turned on the shower. He removed his clothes, leaving them in a pile on the floor, and stepped under the spray, holding out his hand to beckon me.

Joining him, I let Riot wash away the blood. Never had I felt closer to someone. I couldn't help but revel in the power he held over me. It was intoxicating, and my body craved more of his dominance.

Riot took control, pushing me against the wall and thrusting deep inside me. I whimpered in pleasure as he used my body for his own satisfaction, refusing to let me climax until he was ready.

We moved from the wall to the bed where he pinned me down beneath him, his rough hands tracing patterns on my skin that left goose bumps in their wake. He whispered dirty words into my ear.

"My filthy little whore. You like what I do to you, don't you?"

I nodded, unable to lie to him.

"You're mine, Hollis. Every fucking inch of you to do with as I please."

"Yes, yours!"

He growled in approval when I writhed under him, begging for more. His fingers dug into my hips, holding me down as he took me harder and faster than ever before.

I bit my lip to stifle the moans escaping my throat, feeling embarrassingly turned on by his rough handling. The room spun around me in a haze of lust. It was clear we were both lost in this twisted world of desire -- a world where boundaries no longer existed, and pleasure knew no limits.

Through it all, there was one constant thought running through my mind: I never want this to end.

Chapter Nine

Hollis

The key turned in the lock, echoing through the dimly lit secret chamber. I glanced around at the shelves, lined with dust-covered journals and mementos collected from a life of violence and darkness. This was Riot's world, and he had brought me deep into its twisted heart.

"Riot, why did you lock the door?" I asked, trying to keep my voice steady as claustrophobia crept into my chest. I needed an escape plan if things took a turn for the worse. It was hard to trust anyone in Raven's Vale, especially a man like Riot Tredway.

"Because, Hollis," he said, his voice low and menacing as he walked toward one of the bookshelves, "I'm about to show you something no one else has ever seen."

My heart hammered against my ribcage as he pulled a tattered journal from the shelf, the spine creaking under the weight of its dark secrets. Riot dropped it onto a nearby table.

"Read this," he commanded, gesturing to the open journal. His eyes were full of shadows, daring me to look away, but I couldn't. The words on the page were a mirror into his twisted soul, and I found myself drawn to them, unable to resist their perverse allure.

"Jesus, Riot…" I whispered, flipping through the pages filled with violent fantasies and demented ramblings. My hands shook as I read aloud a passage detailing his time in the institute for the criminally insane. "It says here that you witnessed unspeakable horrors during your stay… that they changed you."

"Changed me?" He scoffed, pacing the room like a caged animal. "I was born with the darkness, Hollis.

But the institute… it gave me the opportunity to embrace it fully."

"Sounds terrifying," I murmured, trying to keep the fear from my voice. I knew Riot was dangerous but hearing it straight from him only intensified my dread.

"Terrifying?" he mused, a wicked grin spreading across his face. "No, Hollis, that's not it. It was… liberating."

"Riot, you can't possibly expect me to understand this," I said, closing the journal and setting it down on the table. My heart raced as I looked up at him, searching for some sign of humanity in those cold, unyielding eyes.

"Maybe not," he admitted, his gaze never leaving mine. "But if you're going to stay here with me, you need to know who I am. And what I'm capable of. The journals I showed you before were a mere taste."

And in that moment, despite the fear that gripped my soul, I felt an inexplicable connection to the man standing before me. A bond that was both terrifying and exhilarating in its intensity.

"Crash and Kane," he began, his voice tinged with a twisted fondness. "I met them in the institute. We were all there for… similar reasons. They recognized the darkness within me, just as I saw it in them."

"Darkness?" I echoed, my voice shaking.

"Sadistic desires," he clarified, smirking at my reaction. "An insatiable thirst for blood and pain. We bonded over that shared hunger and became brothers."

"Brothers…" I whispered, trying to comprehend the perverse connection they had formed.

"Brothers," he repeated, his gaze piercing through me. "We promised each other we'd never let anyone control us again. Together, we'd embrace our true nature and rule Raven's Vale with an iron fist."

Riot paused, his expression shifting from pride to something more intense. He clenched his hands into fists, the muscles in his arms tensing as he spoke of a nurse at the institute who dared to show him kindness.

"Her name was Emily," he said. "She thought she could 'save' me. Saw something redeemable in me. Foolish girl."

"What happened to her?" I asked, sensing the tension building within him.

"Her kindness was… intoxicating," he admitted. "For a moment, I allowed myself to be vulnerable with her. To trust her. And then I betrayed her."

I needed to ask, and yet I feared his answer. But still, if I wanted to get closer to Riot and understand him better, I needed to know as much as he was willing to tell me.

"Betrayed her how?" My heart pounded in my chest as I braced myself for the answer.

"By taking her life," he confessed, his eyes burning with a mix of rage and satisfaction. "She never saw it coming. One moment, she was holding my hand, trying to find the humanity in me… and the next, she was lying lifeless on the floor."

"Riot…" I wasn't sure what to say. I knew he enjoyed killing, but to think he'd done it in the institute as well.

"Tell me, Hollis," he demanded, leaning in closer, his breath hot against my cheek. "Can you still look at me knowing what I've done?"

I swallowed hard, torn between the terror that threatened to consume me and the inexplicable bond I felt toward this ruthless killer. In that dimly lit room, I tried to understand the man before me and the darkness that had shaped him.

"Your past is terrifying, Riot," I admitted. "But… I can't deny the connection we have."

He studied me, his cold eyes searching for any hint of deception or weakness. As I met his gaze, all I could do was hope the truth in my words would be enough to satisfy his dark and insatiable hunger.

The dimly lit room seemed to close in on me, the shadows cast by the flickering candles dancing across Riot's face as he continued his story. His words were punctuated with cruel laughter as he described how the nurse had fought for her life, her eyes wide with terror and disbelief.

"Her struggle was pathetic," he sneered, his eyes gleaming with sadistic pleasure. "But I enjoyed every second of it. The way she gasped for air, the way her blood warmed my hands… it was intoxicating."

I shuddered, unable to comprehend the satisfaction he derived from such brutality. My heart raced as I struggled with the realization that this man -- this monster -- was someone I'd grown to care for. And even worse, I was lying to myself. Had I not felt something similar when he'd told me how to kill the man in the alley?

"Is that what you want, Hollis? To be another one of my playthings? To feel my power over you?"

"Riot, I --" I began, but he cut me off, his vulnerability shining through the cracks of his merciless facade.

"Or do you think you can change me?" he asked. "Will you try to save me like she did? But tell me, Hollis… what will you do when you fail?"

My breath caught in my throat as I took in the pain etched across his face. As much as I wanted to deny it, I couldn't ignore that my feelings for Riot went beyond fear and fascination -- there was something deeper, more dangerous lurking beneath the surface.

"Riot, I don't know if I can change you," I admitted, my voice trembling. "But I see something in you that isn't just darkness and violence. There's more to you than that. Maybe it's not that you need to change, and only that you need someone to accept all of you."

His eyes searched mine, a glimmer of hope breaking through the stormy clouds of his soul. For a moment, it felt as if we were standing on the edge of a precipice, teetering between redemption and damnation.

"Will you stay with me, Hollis?" he asked, his voice raw and vulnerable. "Even knowing what I've done -- what I'm capable of?"

I hesitated, my heart pounding as I considered the enormity of the decision before me. Could I really love a man like Riot? A man whose very existence was entwined with death and destruction?

No. It wasn't a matter of whether I *could* because I already did. I'd fallen for him despite everything. Or perhaps because of it.

"Riot," I whispered, reaching out to touch his scarred cheek. "I can't promise that I won't be afraid... but I won't leave you."

As my hand met his skin, something shifted between us -- a connection illuminated by the faintest glimmer of hope. We both knew the path we'd chosen would be fraught with danger and despair, but there was no turning back now.

For better or worse, our fates were intertwined.

I felt Riot's grip on my arm tighten, as if he was trying to hold onto something that was slipping away. I wondered how long he'd waited for someone to see and accept him. Crash and Kane did to some extent, but the fact they couldn't accept my role in Riot's life meant even they only saw part of him.

"Riot, you don't have to prove anything to me. I see you -- I see the complexity beneath the surface."

"And you're the only one who ever has. So don't you dare turn your back on me now."

He released my arm abruptly, and I stumbled back. I knew he was hurting, but the ferocity of his emotions frightened me. Did I really exist in this man's world, or was I merely a pawn?

"Riot, I'm not turning my back on you," I said, trying to keep my voice steady. "But I need you to trust me too. Can you do that? I've done everything I can to show you that I'm not going to leave, that I want to be here with you. And yet, it still seems like it isn't enough for you."

"Trust? You think it's that easy? After everything I've been through, everything I've done? When has anyone ever given me a reason to trust them?"

"What about Crash and Kane?" I asked.

He shrugged. "I don't think any of us completely trust one another. How could we?"

I could see the desperation in his eyes -- the primal need for acceptance, for understanding. And despite my fear, I knew I couldn't leave him.

"I'll stay with you, Riot. But you have to let me in. You have to stop pushing me away when things get tough, or you start feeling emotions you aren't comfortable with."

He stared at me for a moment, as if considering my offer. Then, with a sigh that seemed to carry the weight of a thousand lifetimes, he reached out and pulled me into his arms.

"Okay," he murmured, his voice softening with vulnerability. "I'll try… for you, Hollis."

And so we stood there, two lost souls clinging to each other in the darkness, each trying to find solace in the other's embrace. I didn't know what the future held for us, but for now, it was enough to know that we were not alone.

"You know, I've never experienced love," he admitted, his eyes searching mine for any trace of judgment or pity. "I don't even know what it means, really. But I do know this -- I can't live without you, Hollis. You've become my obsession, my reason for existing."

His words hung in the air between us, raw and vulnerable. I could see the uncertainty in his eyes, the unspoken fear that I would reject him now that he'd laid his heart bare. I took a deep breath, swallowing down the lump that had formed in my throat.

"Riot," I said softly, reaching out to touch his arm. "I think... I think that's how you feel about me. That's love, isn't it? And I... I love you too." I saw the hesitation in his eyes, the way he fought with himself over whether he should believe me or run the other way. "Maybe love is just a word. But whatever it is, I know I care for you, Riot. I don't want to leave your side."

For a moment, he stared at me in silence, his eyes filled with a mixture of disbelief and gratitude. "I never thought I'd hear someone say that to me."

Had his parents never said they loved him? No, probably not. Considering what they'd done to him, I wasn't sure they'd known what love meant. It made me think perhaps he'd been born this way through no fault of his own. Even if his parents hadn't done unspeakable things to him, eventually, the monster within would have emerged.

"Riot," I whispered, my voice barely audible in

the dimly lit room. "Let me show you something different. Something... gentle."

He looked at me, his eyes a stormy sea of uncertainty. I could almost see the gears turning in his head, trying to make sense of what was happening. For a man who'd only known violence and pain, the concept of tenderness seemed foreign to him.

"Fuck, Hollis... I don't know how," he admitted.

"Trust me," I murmured, guiding his free hand to rest upon my cheek. "Just follow my lead."

Our gazes locked, and for a moment, it felt as though we were dancing on the edge of a precipice, teetering between the darkness that had consumed us and the light that promised salvation. And then, with a steadying breath, I leaned forward, pressing my lips against his in a chaste, tender kiss.

It was a simple gesture, but one that held immense power. I could feel Riot's body tense beneath my touch, his pulse quickening at the unfamiliar sensation. Yet, despite his initial resistance, I sensed his resolve crumbling.

"Is this... love?" he asked, his voice barely a whisper, as he hesitantly wrapped his arms around me. It was clear that he struggled to understand the sensations that coursed through him, the myriad of emotions threatening to overwhelm him.

"Maybe," I replied, pressing another gentle kiss to his lips. "Or maybe it's just the beginning of something new for both of us."

I knew that Riot might never fully grasp the complexities of human emotions, that his darkness might always hold sway over him. But as I held him close, feeling the steady rhythm of his heart against my chest, I couldn't help but hope.

Chapter Ten

Riot

Raven's Vale was a cesspool of filth and violence, the perfect breeding ground for someone like me. I'd always fed off the fear that my very name instilled in the hearts of others. But as I sat there, my cold gaze fixed on Hollis, I couldn't help but feel… different.

"Riot," she whispered, her voice trembling with uncertainty. "What's wrong?"

"Nothing," I grunted, trying to shake off the strange sensation gnawing at my insides. Was it love? Or just obsession? I'd never felt anything like this before -- a vulnerability that made me question everything I thought I knew about myself. And I wasn't sure I liked the feeling.

"Look, Hollis," I said, my words edged with frustration. "I wish I could give you the life you deserve. But all I know is pain and destruction. That's who I am. The fucking Butcher. You're never going to get sweet words of affection from me."

She hesitated for a moment before moving closer, her eyes filled with a determined light that caught me off guard. "You've given me more than you realize, Riot," she replied softly, her hand reaching out to brush against my scarred knuckles. "You've shown me a strength I didn't know I had. Let me see a side of you no one else knows about. And I don't need anything else from you."

Her touch ignited a fire within me, one that threatened to consume what little sanity I had left. It terrified me, yet I couldn't bring myself to pull away. My mind raced with unanswered questions and self-doubt -- emotions I wasn't accustomed to. Part of me wanted to lash out, to destroy the very thing I wanted to keep -- Hollis.

"Are you sure about that?" I asked. Not that I was letting her go, but I'd learned something over the years. Even if I didn't react to things the way everyone else would, or feel the same, I'd figured out how to mimic them. As Kane liked to say, I'd figured out how to put on a mask of humanity. "Because once you're in this deep, there's no going back."

"Riot," she murmured, her breath warm against my skin. "There's nowhere else I'd rather be."

My eyes darted to every corner, searching for an escape from the turmoil within me. But there was none. Only Hollis. I felt the need to destroy, to kill. Fisting my hands at my sides, I remained still, refusing to take it out on her. I felt like I needed her, even if I didn't know why.

"Riot... you don't have to be afraid," she whispered, her words piercing through the haze of my thoughts. "I'm not going anywhere."

"Afraid?" I snorted. It wasn't fear I felt. If I thought for one moment she'd run, I'd cuff her to the bed again. I wondered if I could microchip her like a dog, then I'd be able to track her no matter where she went.

It wasn't a bad idea. In fact, now that I'd thought about it, I'd have to get the necessary materials to make it happen. Then I'd know where she was at all times.

My heart thundered in my chest as I stared down at her, my mind racing with a million reasons why toying with her like this was a terrible fucking idea. She was the only one who could make me show a gentler side of myself, even if I knew it was a damn lie. If it's what I needed to do in order to tie her to me even more, then so be it.

I leaned in slowly, tentatively, giving her every

opportunity to pull away. I needed her to want this, to give in to me. By moving slowly, she felt like she had the choice of whether or not to kiss me. Truthfully, if she pulled away, I'd kiss her anyway.

My lips barely touched hers, the lightest kiss I'd ever given. I tried to mimic the things I'd witnessed between couples, the soft touches, loving looks, and sweet kisses. I didn't understand any of it, but I felt like it was necessary right now. Hollis wasn't quite the same as the nurse who'd wanted to save me. However, I had no choice but to consider the fact she wanted to redeem me in some small way or feel like she was special.

She was. Just not in the way she probably thought.

"Riot," she whispered against my lips.

A sound on the other side of the door had me tensing and listening intently. Was it Crash or Kane out there? Possibly both. I couldn't be certain, but it sounded like Lyla's voice -- accompanied by Crash and Kane's sinister laughter. So, those three had been working together just as I'd suspected, even if I didn't know why.

"Riot? What's wrong?" Hollis asked, her gaze searching mine for answers.

"Nothing," I lied, forcing a casual shrug. "Thought I heard something, but it's nothing important."

My mind churned with suspicion, but I couldn't bring myself to reveal what I'd heard. Not now. Not when Hollis was feeling closer to me than ever before. I could tell in the way she touched me, the soft smile curving her lips. Even if I didn't know what love was, it was clear that's what she thought she felt for me, and I'd use that if I needed to.

"Okay," she said, though I could tell she didn't quite believe me. She leaned against my chest, resting her head on my shoulder as we sat in silence.

I couldn't shake the nagging feeling in the back of my mind that something was off. The thought of Lyla being tangled up with Crash and Kane made my blood boil. Those two motherfuckers had caused nothing but pain and suffering in Raven's Vale, same as me. I knew they'd only use Lyla for their own twisted purposes. But I also knew that dragging Hollis into this mess would only put her at risk, and I'd be damned if I let anything hurt her. If someone was going to put a mark on her, it would be me.

"Hey," I muttered. "What do you say we get out of here for a while? Maybe go somewhere quiet, just the two of us."

That's the sort of thing women liked, wasn't it? A date of sorts? It wasn't like I'd ever been in a relationship before. Never wanted one. I wanted to control Hollis. Possess her. Bind her to me in every way possible so that she voluntarily stayed with me. And not once would she suspect I'd backed her into a corner and put a collar on her.

"Really?" Hollis asked, her face lighting up with surprise and excitement. "You'd want to do that?"

"Sure," I said, forcing a smile. "Why the fuck not?"

"Sounds perfect," she agreed, squeezing my hand as we rose to our feet.

As we stepped out into the dimly lit hallway, my ears strained for any sign of Lyla, Crash, and Kane. But all I heard was the distant echo of our own footsteps. Whatever they'd been doing, it seemed they'd moved elsewhere.

"Riot," Hollis whispered, her fingers still

intertwined with mine, "Thank you."

I didn't know what the fuck she was thanking me for -- all I'd done was drag her deeper into the darkness that consumed me. But in that moment, I knew one thing for certain: I'd do anything to keep her safe, even if it meant facing off against the men I considered my brothers. For the first time in my life, I had something that was mine and only mine, and I'd never let her go.

"Is it really safe for us to leave this place?" Hollis asked. "You have to stay in Raven's Vale, don't you?"

I paused. To some extent, she was right. If I was caught outside of town, then I'd end up back in the hell I'd escaped from. Unless they sent me to prison. And as for this small town, there weren't a lot of places I could take her.

"What about a drink?" I asked.

"You mean at the bar?"

"Why not?" I took her hand and led her out of the house and down the street. The bar I had in mind wasn't far. Raven's Vale actually had two, but the one I preferred was in the seedier part of town. Of course, no one was going to fuck with me regardless of where I went.

We entered the establishment and Hollis stared at everything with wide eyes. Clearly, she'd never been here before. I wasn't really surprised. It didn't seem like her sort of place.

I led her up to the bar and motioned for her to sit on a stool, and I claimed the one beside her. The bartender came over, arms crossed, and glowered at me. We'd had run-ins a few times before, but I let his attitude slide -- most of the time.

"Beer for me," I said.

"And you?" he asked Hollis.

She licked her lips. "Um. Something fruity?"

The bartender snorted. "Do we look like we offer froufrou drinks? Sorry, but your options are beer, vodka, whiskey, or rum."

"Rum and coke?" she asked, sounding uncertain. Obviously she'd never had it before. I had a feeling tonight would be interesting.

While she was distracted by everything going on around us, I noticed someone in the corner who could get me what I needed. I placed a hand on Hollis' shoulder and leaned in to whisper to her. "Stay put. I'll be right back."

She tensed but gave me a nod. I hurried over to Ben and sat across from him.

"And what does The Butcher need tonight?" Ben asked. "Drugs? I doubt it's sex since you came in with a woman."

"Neither. I need to get my hands on a GPS I can inject into her. I need to know where she is every second of the day. Can it be done?"

Ben leaned back and sighed. "Yeah, but it won't be cheap. They won't give a shit who you are, or why you want it, but they *will* want cold hard cash for it."

"I want it tonight. Get the money from the dear ol' mayor, then drop it off at the mansion. Make sure you bring it to my room. I don't trust Crash or Kane with it."

He nodded. "Consider it done. Might be late, though. And you'll have to use that computer you hate so much, or your phone. It will be the only way to keep track of her."

"Fine. Just get it to me." I stood and went back to Hollis. She'd already started sipping her drink, and I couldn't help but laugh at the look on her face. Her nose wrinkled, and she faked a gag after every swallow. I drained half my beer and watched her. She managed to finish her drink and I got her another. If I was going to chip her like a wayward puppy, then it might be better if she were drunk off her ass first.

Although, the idea of her fighting back and having to restrain her excited me. I loved her spirit. Even when I could see the fear in her eyes, she didn't back down. She'd done her best to face me head-on, and not many people in this town could do such a thing. It was part of why she fascinated me.

I'd given her glimpses of my past, told her a few sob stories. It didn't take much to make her sympathize with me. I'd twist and mold her into the perfect woman to remain by my side. But there was only so much I could do... If Hollis hadn't already had a darker side, then I never could have convinced her to kill anyone.

Once she'd had enough to drink that she could barely stand, I lifted her into my arms and carried her home. Stripping off her clothes, I cuffed her to the bed. She was so out of it, she didn't even question why I'd done it.

By the time Ben arrived with the tracker, Hollis had been asleep for more than an hour. I took the items from him, listened to his quick explanation, and then dismissed him. After I locked the door, I prepped the tracker and then inserted it in her thigh, just under her ass cheek.

Rubbing the lump, I hoped she wouldn't notice it, or that it would burrow deeper on its own. It wouldn't do me any good for someone to spot it and draw her attention to it. Then again, if she wore something short enough for them to spot it, I'd have to kill whoever saw her that way. And as they said, dead men couldn't tell tales. I'd found a blade across their throat was an excellent way to silence someone.

"Sweet dreams, Hollis." I took off my clothes and wrapped myself around her. Breathing in her scent, I closed my eyes and smiled a little. I'd been taming her a bit at a time, and she hadn't even realized it.

Now that I had Hollis right where I wanted her, I'd have to deal with Crash and Kane... but that was a problem for another day. For now, I'd enjoy watching the different emotions play across Hollis' face. From fear to excitement to hope and even what I assumed was love... with Hollis, every day brought something new. I didn't think I'd ever grow bored of her, but if I did... Well, I'd cross that bridge when I came to it.

Chapter Eleven

Hollis

Riot had been gone for hours, and I could no longer wait for him. Making my way downstairs, I listened intently, hoping Crash and Kane were gone as well. I tried not to leave the room without Riot, but I hadn't eaten lunch, and it was now nearing dinnertime. There was no way of knowing when Riot would return, and I was starving.

"Going somewhere, Hollis?" Crash asked from behind me.

I tensed and glanced over my shoulder, seeing both him and Kane. Before I had a chance to second-guess myself, I bolted. I knew it wasn't likely I could escape them, but I had to at least try. I didn't make it far before Crash wrapped his arms around me, yanking me up off the floor.

"Get off me!" I screamed, struggling to break free from his grasp. But he was too strong.

"Riot won't save you this time," Crash whispered into my ear, his words making my blood run cold. They dragged me through the house and out onto the streets.

I didn't dare scream. For one, it wouldn't do me any good. Not unless Riot was nearby. And second, it might draw unwanted attention. What if Crash and Kane had people out here waiting to help in the event I did manage to get past them? I could barely hold on as it was. If anyone else decided to take a few swings, or worse, I wasn't sure I'd last.

They forced me to keep moving, not stopping until we'd reached the edge of town. In the distance, a building loomed ahead, its decaying walls seeming to mock me with their crumbling facade. As we entered the derelict structure, horror began to twist its tendrils around my heart. What did they want from me? Why had they brought me here?

Crash shoved me into a chair, the rickety wood groaning beneath me as they bound my wrists and ankles with coarse rope that bit into my flesh, drawing blood. Panic surged through me as I realized there was no escape -- not from these sadistic monsters, nor from the terror that threatened to swallow me whole.

"Comfortable?" Kane snickered, circling me like a predator sizing up its prey.

"Fuck you!" I couldn't let them see how scared I was right now. I knew that would only make things worse.

"Feisty little thing, aren't you?" Crash remarked, smirking cruelly. "Riot must've had his hands full."

"Leave him out of this."

"Sorry, sweetheart." Kane leaned in close. "But you're our ticket to breaking him. And we won't hesitate to do whatever it takes to get what we want from you. Crash and I may be killers, but we're different from Riot. Not once have I detected any humanity in that bastard."

My heart pounded violently against my ribcage. I couldn't let them win. No matter what they did to me, I had to protect Riot, even if it cost me everything. What would they do to him if they discovered he treated me gently? It was one thing for them to think he'd grown attached to me, but I doubt he'd ever shown a tender side to either of them.

The flickering fluorescent light overhead cast ghastly shadows on Crash and Kane's faces as they loomed over me. A cold sweat clung to my skin. I had a feeling I wasn't getting out of here. Not alive at any rate. Would Riot be the one to find my lifeless body?

"Tell us, Hollis. What the fuck did you do to him? Why hasn't he killed you like all the others?"

"Nothing!" I cried out. "I didn't do anything."

"Riot's never given a damn about anyone before," Kane said, pacing with restless energy. "So why the hell would he start caring about some pathetic little bitch like you? From what I can see, there's nothing special about you."

"I don't have to tell you shit." I glared at them. If I could just keep them talking, then maybe Riot would return and realize something was wrong.

"Watch your mouth, girl," Crash warned. "Or we'll find a way to keep it shut for you."

"Go ahead and try." I refused to give them the satisfaction of breaking me, even if every fiber of my being screamed for me to run as far as I could and hide from these two.

"Have it your way." Kane cracked his knuckles. "But don't say we didn't warn you."

"Riot won't let you get away with this."

"Believe what you want, sweetheart," Crash mocked, leaning in close so his breath washed over me. "But Riot's not going to save you. Nobody is. You can scream, and no one will come running. Beg and plead all you like. We don't care."

"Riot will kill you both," I whispered. "And I'll be there to watch you bleed."

Although, I had to wonder if he really would. He considered Crash and Kane his family. What if his loyalty to them ran deeper than what we had together? He might have done his best to keep me safe from them so far, but it didn't mean he'd slaughter them for hurting me.

"Now, let's get down to business, shall we?" Crash asked.

The glint of a knife caught my eye, its cold steel reflecting the light that flickered in the room. Crash drew it from his belt, twirling it between his fingers with unnerving ease.

"I personally prefer guns," he said. "I'm not into messy and bloody like Riot is, but for you, I'll make an exception. Shall we see how tough you really are?"

"You can both go to hell," I said.

"Wrong answer." I felt the first searing pain as Crash sliced into the flesh of my arm. I bit my lip to suppress a scream, unwilling to give them any satisfaction. The blood began to flow, warm and sticky against my skin. I could hear the sound of it dripping onto the floor, even over the roaring in my ears.

"Ready to talk now?" Crash asked, his eyes gleaming with sadistic delight.

I gritted my teeth against the agony and shook my head. No matter what they did, I couldn't give in. If Riot came and saw that I'd relented, he'd be disappointed in me. I needed to be strong.

"Suit yourself," he replied, tracing the knife across my other arm in a slow, agonizing cut. I couldn't hold back the cry of pain this time, and both Crash and Kane laughed cruelly at my suffering.

"Still think Riot's coming for you?" Kane taunted, leaning in close to whisper in my ear. "Trust me, he's long gone by now. Off on a kill most likely. I've been watching, and he seemed a bit antsy."

I fought against my restraints, the ropes biting into my wrists as I struggled to free myself. Every movement sent fresh waves of pain shooting through my body, but I refused to give up. I would not let them break me.

"Is that all you've got?" I glared defiantly at Crash. "You're going to have to do better than that if you want to make me talk."

"But don't worry -- we've got plenty more in store for you." Crash kneeled in front of me, twirling the knife again. What the hell did they have planned?

He sank the blade into my thigh, and I nearly blacked out. The sound of it being pulled out nearly made me sick.

"Riot will find you," I said, clenching my teeth, my vision swimming as the pain became almost unbearable. "And when he does, you'll wish you'd never laid a hand on me."

"Keep dreaming, sweetheart."

Kane came closer again, slapping my face with his open palm. My head whipped to the side and pain bloomed across my face. A tear slid down my cheek, and I heard him snicker. *Asshole*!

But even as my body racked with agony, my mind clung to one unwavering thought -- that Riot would come, and he would save me from this nightmare. Blood dripped from my split lip. Kane's fist slammed into my stomach, and I coughed and sputtered, gasping for breath. I could feel the sting of each bruise and cut that marred my skin.

"Still not talking?" Crash asked, his fist connecting with my cheek. The impact sent a jolt of pain through my skull, and I tasted blood as I bit down on my tongue to keep from crying out. Even if Riot did come for me, I wasn't going to look very pretty. Who knew how long it would take to heal from everything they'd done to me already, much less whatever else they were going to do.

They wanted answers, but I wouldn't break. I couldn't. My loyalty to Riot was unwavering, even in the face of this torture. It didn't matter if he was able to love me back. I'd fallen for him, and I wouldn't betray him.

"Feisty bitch," Kane muttered, yanking my head back by my hair. "But she won't last much longer. We still have a few aces up our sleeves."

"Riot's going to tear you apart for this. You've said it yourself. I clearly mean something to him." My words were slurring, and my vision blurred. I hoped I could stay awake.

Crash chuckled darkly, his sadistic glee evident in every syllable. "We'll see about that. As long as you're alive, it means we have leverage. If he really does think you're something special, then he'll do what we want if it means keeping you alive."

"What you want?" I asked. "I thought you just wanted me dead."

Crash shrugged. "Yes and no. We've left Riot in charge for a handful of reasons."

Kane snorted. "Yeah, like he's crazier than either of us."

Crash shot him a glare. "But if Riot really does care for you, then he'd do anything to get you back."

"Let's try something else," Kane suggested, grabbing a rusty pair of pliers from a nearby table. He approached me slowly, a sinister smile playing across his lips.

I couldn't hold on much longer. What was he going to do with those? Fear filled me, and I struggled to not let the darkness creep in and suck me down. Who knew what they'd do if I passed out?

"Such a brave little thing," Kane taunted, gripping one of my fingers tightly with the pliers. "But let's see how long that lasts."

The pressure increased, and every ounce of my resolve shattered as the pain became unbearable. I screamed, my body shaking with agony and terror, but still, I refused to give them what they wanted. The pliers bit into my finger, breaking the skin and cracking the bone.

"What did you do to him? Why does he give a shit about you?" Crash asked.

I couldn't have answered if I wanted to. My mind felt fuzzy, and if I hadn't been tied to the chair, I'd have fallen to the floor by now. Only the ropes were holding me up.

Kane applied even more pressure to my finger. White hot pain hit me, and I screamed long and loud, no longer able to hold back. Tears flowed freely, but I wouldn't beg for mercy. I knew they didn't have any to give.

My head lolled to the side, vision nearly going black from the pain coursing through my body. I forced myself to focus on my surroundings, searching for any possible escape plan or weakness I could exploit to turn the tables on Crash and Kane. With the damage they'd done to my body, I wasn't sure I could escape even if I were free.

They continued their sadistic work, and I gritted my teeth, forcing my mind to go elsewhere, someplace warm and safe. Whatever came next, I wasn't sure I wanted to be fully present for it. If they knew Riot at all, then they'd have realized this was a terrible idea. Even if I died, I didn't think they would get out of this unscathed. I might not be around to see it happen, but Riot would get revenge for me.

"I'm not sure why he thinks she's so amazing," Kane said. "Seems like all the others. Weak. She'll break eventually."

Never. No matter how much they tortured me, or what they said, I wouldn't give in. Every blow, every insult broke me down a little at a time, and yet, I managed to hold on.

"He's going to be so pissed," I murmured.

"You'll either be dead when he gets here, or close to it. Even if he comes back and realizes you're gone, he still has to find you. This town may not be big, but there are tons of places we could have taken you." Crash smiled. "But until then, I'm sure we can squeeze in a few more hours of playtime. You're up for it, right, Hollis?"

"Count on it." I barely got the words out and couldn't hold my head up. I knew they had to find me funny. Talking all brave and acting like none of this mattered -- when they were clearly winning.

"Look, Hollis. I believe you have a visitor," Kane said.

I managed to move my head enough to look toward the door. Had Riot come for me? My breath froze in my lungs when I saw Lyla heading toward me. How had she known where I was? Had she come to save me? No, the way she smiled at me reeked of evil and madness. She really had been working with Crash and Kane all along.

"Look who's here," Crash sneered as Lyla walked in hesitantly. My heart dropped like a stone when I realized she was part of this cruel game.

"What's the matter? Surprised your little friend turned on you?" Kane asked. "She's been our little gopher for a while now. Long before Riot took a liking to you. She's not bad for a quick fuck either."

My body trembled and bile rose in my throat, but I focused all my remaining energy on keeping my gaze locked on Lyla. "Why, Lyla? I thought we were friends."

She scoffed, finally meeting my gaze. "You really think anyone could be friends with a pathetic piece of shit like you? Pretending to like you was awful. I couldn't stand listening to you, much less spending time together."

Tears streamed down my face. The pain in my battered body paled in comparison to the bitter sting of her words. All this time, I'd managed to get through every day of my miserable life because I thought I had a friend. Someone who understood, who cared. It had all been a lie. Was my entire life meaningless?

"Time's almost up, Hollis," Crash said. "Last chance to spill before things get really ugly."

But just as despair threatened to consume me, a distant noise caught my attention. It was faint, but unmistakable -- a heavy thud that sounded like approaching footsteps.

"R-Riot?" My heart hammered in my chest. Please let it be him!

"Ha! You're delusional," Lyla snorted, but I saw a flicker of doubt in her eyes. "He'd never come here. Not for you. Don't tell me you thought he really wanted you? I knew you were pathetic, but really?"

"What if he is here?" I asked.

"Keep dreaming, bitch." Lyla laughed as Kane stepped closer, pressing a knife to my throat. Was this the end? Were they going to slice my neck and let me bleed out?

"Ticktock, Hollis," Crash warned, an evil grin stretching across his face. "Time's running out. Why does Riot keep you around? How are you making him change?"

"I was never your friend, Hollis. Just another pawn in this fucked-up game," Lyla said. "I used you, and I'm sure Riot is too. You have no one but yourself in this entire world. Why are you fighting so hard? Just give in already."

"He's coming," I whispered, knowing deep in my gut that what I'd said was true.

Lyla shook her head. "You're hearing things, Hollis. No one is coming for you. Remember when I told you I'd help you find a way out of Raven's Vale? I lied. I never wanted you to leave. I just wanted to see the hope in your eyes die, watch you wither a little more every day."

Lyla leaned in close. The look in her eyes screamed *I'm a crazy person*. How had I never noticed it before?

"Every time you confided in me, every secret you shared... I told them all to Crash and Kane. They've known your every hope and dream, your every fear since the beginning."

"You're a monster," I whispered, unable to hold back a sob.

"Look who's talking, sweetheart," Lyla shot back, her eyes glinting with cruel amusement. "You really think you're any better than us? You're in love with a fucking serial killer. How screwed up is that?"

"Time's up." Crash was ready to make good on his threats. If Riot didn't get in here soon, I was going to die.

The door exploded inward, shattering into a storm of splinters. Riot stood there, his towering frame wreathed in shadows, his eyes blazing with fury.

"Step away from her." His voice sounded like a deadly promise.

In that moment, as if sensing her own doom, Lyla made a run for it. She sprinted toward the shattered doorway, but Riot was faster. With one swift motion, he closed the distance, catching her by the throat. His blade flashed, slicing through flesh and tendon, and Lyla crumpled to the ground, choking on her own blood.

"Riot." Relief and terror warred within me as he turned his attention to Crash and Kane. I'd been right. He'd come for me.

His hands fisted at his sides as he advanced toward Crash and Kane, his boots thudding against the filthy floor. "You two should've known better than to fuck with what's mine."

"Riot, man, we were just --" Kane didn't get to finish his sentence before Riot's fist connected with his jaw, silencing him. The force of the blow sent Kane sprawling, blood spraying from his mouth as he hit the ground.

"Shut the fuck up! I told the two of you before. Hands off. What the hell did you do to her?" Riot asked.

I watched from my chair, bound and bruised, as something fierce and terrible bloomed within me at the sight of Riot defending me. A love so twisted that it hurt yet felt so right. This man, this monster, was willing to spill blood for me. The blood of his brothers at that. The two people who had been the closest to him. And I knew, without a doubt, that I would do the same for him.

"Please, Riot, let's talk about this." Crash backed away as Riot stalked toward him.

"Talk? There's nothing to talk about." He lunged at Crash, grabbing him by the throat and slamming him against the wall. His eyes burned with a sadistic fire as he tightened his grip, and I wondered if he might actually kill Crash.

"Tell me, Crash. Did you really think you could get away with hurting her? Did you honestly believe you could break us apart?"

Crash wheezed, struggling for air. His hands

clawed at Riot's, trying to pry himself free.

"Fucking pathetic." Riot released Crash's throat only to slam his fist into his gut, doubling him over in agony.

I could hardly breathe as I watched Riot tear through them. It scared me how much I loved him in this moment, his brutal strength and savage devotion. I'd never wanted anyone more.

"Riot," I whispered, my voice barely audible above the sounds of violence and pain. "They're your family. Don't kill them."

He glanced back at me, a wicked grin spreading across his face. "Don't have to kill them to make a point."

His fist slammed into Crash's temple, knocking him out with one blow. Kane didn't even resist as Riot hit him again and again. Once he passed out, Riot came over to untie me. The moment the bonds were loosened, I fell into Riot's arms, unable to sit upright.

My tears soaked his shirt as he lifted me and carried me out of the building. I was finally safe. Or as safe as I'd ever be as long as I remained by his side.

Chapter Twelve

Riot

Blood stained my hands as I cradled Hollis in my arms, carrying her out of the building. Every bruise and cut on her body felt like a personal failure. This was my fault. I should've protected her better. But now, she was hurt, and I knew she wouldn't heal without medical attention.

"Fuck," I muttered, trying to catalog her injuries as I moved swiftly through the dark streets of Raven's Vale. The cold night air stung my face, but it couldn't compare to the burning rage consuming me.

"Please don't die on me, Hollis," I whispered, tightening my grip on her limp form. "You're not getting off that easy."

I stormed into the doctor's home, kicking the door off its hinges as I entered. The sound echoed through the house.

"Doctor!" I bellowed. My voice boomed through the quiet space. "Get your ass down here!"

The woman appeared at the top of the stairs, her eyes wide with fear as she took in the sight before her. Good. Fear was what kept these people in line.

"Help her." My gaze locked onto hers. "If she dies, you'll wish you'd never been born."

The threat hung heavy in the air. I heard the doctor audibly swallow and saw the way her hand trembled as she gripped the railing.

"Y-yes, Mr. Tredway," the doctor stammered, hurrying down the stairs. I could see the desperation in her eyes as she tried to prepare for whatever horrors awaited her.

"Riot," I corrected her sharply. "My old man was Mr. Tredway, and I refuse to be associated with him. I only keep his name to remind me of the hell I endured."

"Right… Riot." She swallowed hard. "I'll do my best."

"You better pray your best is good enough." I watched her every move. She had no idea just how close she was to her own destruction. And if she didn't save Hollis, she'd find out firsthand.

Let her live. For once in my miserable existence, let me have this one fucking thing.

I followed the doctor into her home office. The cold metal of the examination table sent a shiver down my spine as I gently laid Hollis on it. Her fragile form seemed so out of place in this sterile room. The doctor hovered nearby, her eyes darting between Hollis and me as she tried to gauge just how close to the edge I was.

"Start fixing her," I said, my voice icy and hard.

"Y-yes, Riot," the doctor stuttered, scrambling to gather her instruments. She approached Hollis cautiously, as if she were a ticking time bomb ready to go off at any moment. And maybe she was -- because if anything went wrong, I'd make damn sure there'd be an explosion the likes of which Raven's Vale had never seen.

As the doctor worked frantically to stabilize Hollis, I paced the length of the room, each step echoing like a gunshot in the otherwise quiet space. My impatience grew with every passing second, a mounting pressure inside me threatening to erupt in a storm of violence. My gaze never wavered from Hollis.

The smell of antiseptic filled the air as I watched the doctor work, each stitch she made on Hollis' skin igniting a burning rage within me. My eyes lingered on every bruise and cut marring her body, fury building with each new injury I discovered. Damn Crash and Kane to hell -- I should have made them suffer ten times worse for what they did to her.

"Are you almost fucking done?" I asked, my fists clenching by my sides. The doctor flinched, her hands shaking as she tried to steady her needle. "Hurry the hell up."

"Almost... done," she whispered, beads of sweat forming on her brow. "I'm doing my best."

"Your best better be enough," I said, my glare drilling into her. "Or I'll rip you apart limb by limb, and that's a fucking promise. Remember, Doc -- if she dies, you die. Keep that in mind when you're stitching her up."

With that, I turned my attention back to Hollis, my gaze softening ever so slightly as I took in her battered form. She was alive, for now. And I'd make sure she stayed that way, no matter what it took.

The doctor nodded once, her hands steadying as she finished tending to Hollis' wounds. I could tell she knew just how serious my threat was -- and that it wasn't an idle one.

"All right," she said at last, stepping back from the table, her eyes never leaving mine. "Her vitals are stabilizing. She's out of immediate danger, but she'll need ongoing care. I've done everything I can for now. I'd recommend putting her in the hospital, but I don't think you want that."

"You're right, I don't," I replied.

The last time I let Hollis out of sight, my brothers had tried to kill her. Fuck if I was going to let the hospital take care of her when I couldn't remain her with her twenty-four-seven. Not without freeing up some hospital beds by sending a few patients to the morgue. No, if I was going to lose my shit right now,

I'd better do it at home and aim it at the two men who deserved it.

I owed Crash and Kane a lot more pain than I'd already inflicted. I wouldn't kill them. After all, they helped maintain the status quo in this town. Handling it all on my own wouldn't be easy and would take me away from Hollis even more.

My gaze shifted back to Hollis, her face pale and fragile beneath the dim light of the room. She looked so vulnerable. The sight stirred something deep inside me, a fierce protectiveness that threatened to consume everything else.

What the fuck was wrong with me? Possessive, I understood. Why did I feel the need to protect her? Because she belonged to me? I hoped that's all it was. I didn't have time for soft emotions like love or any of that romantic shit. Quickest way to ruin a man.

I allowed myself a small, bitter smile as I stared down at Hollis. She was still alive, and I intended to keep it that way. And as for Crash and Kane? They'd pay, in blood and agony, for every mark they'd left on her. That much, I swore.

* * *

The moon glared down at me as I carried Hollis through the night, her body limp and fragile in my arms. The mansion loomed ahead, its darkened windows telling me Crash and Kane weren't there -- or were hiding from me.

I carried Hollis up to our room and laid her down on the bed with a gentleness that would've shocked those who knew me only as The Butcher. My fingers brushed against her bruised skin as I tucked her in, the contrast between my callused hands and her delicate frame striking me more than ever before. I'd kill anyone who dared to touch her again. She was mine. If anyone was going to cause her pain, it would be me.

"Riot… we need to talk," Crash's voice cut through my thoughts, and I glanced up to see him and Kane standing in the doorway, their eyes locked on Hollis.

"Are you sure that's wise?" I asked.

"Look, man, we fucked up," Crash began, his usual smugness replaced by something almost resembling remorse. "We didn't know she meant so much to you. We won't touch her again."

I got the feeling he was lying through his teeth, but I'd let it slide for now. As long as they knew to never touch Hollis again, that would be enough. If there was more going on, I'd deal with it later.

"Damn right you won't. You so much as breathe in her direction, and I'll make sure your last moments on this earth are filled with more pain than you can even fucking imagine." I flexed my hands. "As it is, I want to beat the shit out of both of you again. I don't think you've suffered enough."

"Understood," Kane mumbled, his gaze shifting nervously between me and Hollis. "We thought she was making you soft."

"Soft? Why?" I asked.

"You're different with her," Crash said. "It's like you care or something."

He wasn't entirely wrong. I did feel something for her, even if I couldn't define it. But telling them that would only cause more problems. "She belongs to me. You touched my property, tried to kill her, and you thought I'd be fine with it? You know how I am about my possessions. Now get the fuck out of here before I decide to carve a few inches off both your hides."

As they turned away, I couldn't help but wonder

what kind of sick game fate was playing with me. A monster like me shouldn't feel this way about anyone, least of all a woman as innocent as Hollis. Sure, I called her my property. I definitely obsessed over her. Even I could admit as much. But the fact it could possibly be something more was the one thing I didn't like and would never admit.

As I watched her sleep, her chest rising and falling with each shallow breath, I knew one thing for certain: there was no going back. She was mine now, and I'd be damned if I let anyone take her from me.

* * *

It had been a week and Hollis had slept through most of it. When she was awake, I gave her pain medication, soup, and made sure she stayed hydrated. All the things the doctor said she'd need in order to survive.

The doctor's visits had become a daily routine, and each time she entered the mansion, I wondered if she'd end up telling me bad news. Hollis didn't seem to be recovering as quickly as I'd have liked. Even the doctor had looked concerned over a few of the wounds.

"Riot," the doctor murmured, her voice trembling as she approached Hollis. "I need to examine her."

"Make it quick, and don't fuck up." It had become my mantra whenever the doctor showed up.

The doctor nodded, her hands shaking as she began examining Hollis. My gaze never wavered, my eyes boring into her every movement, ensuring that she didn't screw up and cause more harm than good.

"Her condition is better, and she's still stable, but she needs more time to recover."

"Every day she's like this, she's vulnerable. Tell

me, is she going to fucking die?"

"Riot, I can't predict the future. She's weak, but she's fighting. Her wounds *are* healing, even if it's slow. I'm doing everything I can to help her," the doctor replied.

"Then do more, or I swear to God…" I trailed off, not needing to finish the threat. I could see the fear in her eyes, and knew she understood the consequences all too well.

As more days passed, I found myself growing increasingly restless. It wasn't just her survival at stake. It was mine as well. I'd never been one for sentimentality or attachment, but I couldn't deny the hold Hollis had over me. And as I watched her, clinging to life, I began to realize just how much I needed her.

"Riot," she murmured, her voice weaker than I'd have liked.

"Hey," I said softly, my voice surprisingly gentle. "How are you feeling?"

"Like hell," she replied, attempting a weak smile. "But I'm still here."

"Damn right, you are," I muttered, my eyes never leaving hers. "And I'll make sure you stay that way."

* * *

The first time I saw Hollis sit up in bed, the relief hit me like a sucker punch to the gut. Her eyes, once glassy and distant, now held a spark of life that sent my heart racing.

"Riot." She held out her hand to me. "I feel so much better. Thank you for taking care of me."

"About fucking time," I replied gruffly. But even as I spoke, my hand moved instinctively to brush a strand of hair from her face -- a touch so tender it almost surprised me.

"Careful, you might actually start acting like a human being," Hollis teased, her lips twitching into a weak smile. My own mouth quirked in response, though I couldn't quite bring myself to return the sentiment.

"Fuck off," I muttered, though the words held no real venom. They were more an admission of defeat than anything else. Because as much as I hated to admit it, Hollis had wormed her way under my skin, and there was no denying the possessive need that had taken root within me.

I'd thought things were finally better, and we were heading back to our normal lives when the doctor arrived that day with a clipboard clutched tightly in her trembling hands. I could sense that something was off -- and I didn't like it one bit.

"Spit it out. What's wrong with her?"

"Riot... I ran some tests while treating Hollis." The doctor hesitated, her eyes darting between us before finally settling on me. "She's pregnant."

For a moment, the world seemed to go silent, leaving nothing but the sound of blood pounding in my ears. Then, without warning, a primal rage surged through me, and I lashed out, my fist connecting with the wall beside the doctor's head.

"You're fucking lying," I snarled. "Dr. Fields informed me I can't have children. So there's no fucking way Hollis is pregnant."

"Riot, please," the doctor stammered, her eyes wide with terror. "The results are clear. I only ran a pregnancy test because I realized there was more to your relationship, and certain drugs could harm a baby."

"Get out!" I roared, grabbing her by the collar

and shoving her toward the door. "Get the fuck out of here before I put your head through the Goddamn wall!"

And just like that, she was gone -- leaving me alone with Hollis and the bitter taste of betrayal.

"Riot?" Hollis murmured, her eyes searching mine for answers. But all I could do was stare back at her, my heart a twisted knot of pain and anger.

"Did you know?" I asked finally, my voice hoarse. "Did you keep this from me?"

"Riot, I swear, I didn't know," she whispered, tears brimming in her eyes. "I --"

"Save it," I spat, cutting her off. "Just... fucking save it."

As I stormed out of the room, my hands trembling with rage, one thought echoed through my mind: someone was going to pay for this, and they were going to pay dearly. If she was pregnant and it wasn't mine, then someone had dared to touch what belonged to me.

* * *

The air was thick with the scent of fear as I strode into Dr. Fields' office, my fists clenched and rage boiling beneath the surface. This was the woman who had sworn, years ago, that I couldn't have children -- a fact I'd accepted without question until now.

"Riot Tredway," she stammered, her face paling at the sight of me. "What brings you here?"

"Cut the shit, Nora." I slammed my hands down on her desk. "You fucking lied to me."

"Wh-what do you mean?" she asked, beads of sweat forming on her brow. Yeah, I could nearly taste her fear. She either knew exactly why I was so pissed, or she'd lied to me about multiple things and wasn't sure exactly how fucked she was right now.

"Your little lie just cost someone dearly." I narrowed my eyes. "Hollis is pregnant, and you're going to tell me how the fuck that's possible when you swore I was sterile."

"Riot, I can assure you, my initial diagnosis was accurate," she insisted, her voice shaking. "I don't know what happened, but --"

"Wrong answer." I grabbed her by the collar and lifted her off her feet. As I slammed her against the wall, I could feel the rush of power coursing through my veins. "Think very carefully about your next words, Doctor."

"Please, Riot," she begged, struggling for breath as I tightened my grip. "There may be... other factors... I didn't consider before. You might not be entirely sterile, just... less likely to --"

"Less likely?" I asked, my voice dripping with disdain. "You told me it was impossible. Not difficult. *Impossible*. And now there's a child growing inside Hollis, a life I never wanted but won't hesitate to protect, simply because she seems like the type who'd want to keep it."

"Riot, I'm sorry," she choked out. "I should have been more thorough --"

"Damn right, you should have. Or maybe it wasn't a case of being wrong. Perhaps you've been lying to me all along, about this and who knows what else. Remember what I told you in the very beginning? Betray me and I'd make your life hell?"

I pulled her away from the wall only to slam her against it again. I heard her teeth snap together from the impact, and hoped I'd caused her at least a little bit of pain. Much more was coming her way, though.

I pulled out my phone and called Kane, putting it on speaker.

"Hello," Kane said when the call connected.

"Need you at Nora Fields' office. Bring Crash. If the two of you want to make up for the shit you pulled, here's your chance." I ended the call, not even waiting for his response. I knew he'd come. Both of them would.

"It's your lucky day, Doc. You get the buy one, get one free special. Not only is Kane going to fuck up your world, but Crash is too. Aren't you lucky? You really should thank me." I smiled. "After all, I'd do far worse things to you than either of them, and you know it."

She choked and gasped, clawing at my hand. I held her in place, pinned to the wall, until Crash and Kane arrived. They took one look at my face and the doc and knew something had gone wrong.

"This bitch has been lying to me. She's probably lied to the two of you as well," I said.

"What did she lie about?" Kane asked.

"She said I was sterile. I'm not." I let my words sink in. "Hollis is pregnant."

"What purpose did it serve to tell him that?" Kane asked. "Were you hoping he'd knock someone up?"

Nora sagged and gave a bark of humorless laughter. "Fine. Looks like I'm caught. Want to know the truth? The three of you were perfect research for a paper I wanted to write about the mental and physical qualities of serial killers. And I may have thought one of you having a kid would be golden. Then I could study it from the time it was born and see if it turned out like any of you regardless of whether it had a loving home. I could have documented every detail of the child's life as it was happening."

"You think we'd love our children?" I asked.

"Not you. Their mothers. Even if one or two of you kept your kids, I knew at least one of the three would discard them. That child could be brought up in a normal home. No abuse. Just love and affection." Dr. Fields smiled, as if she thought it was the most brilliant idea ever.

Crash shot me a look. "Maybe it's just me, but it seems like she's confessing a little too quickly. Besides, her logic is flawed."

"On many levels," Kane muttered.

"What made you think we wouldn't just kill the women carrying our kids?" Crash asked. "Did it not occur to you none of us want families? We aren't the domestic type."

Dr. Fields' brow furrowed. "But Riot hasn't killed Hollis. So I was right, wasn't I?"

"I can't pretend to understand what's going on with Riot and Hollis, and I'm not sure he knows either," Kane said. "But the baby has nothing to do with the fact she's still breathing. More than likely, any women you sent to us would have died the same day we fucked them."

"Ha! My plan was so much more involved than that. Do you take me for an amateur?" Her eyes were feverish as she told us everything she'd planned. As much as I wanted to snap her neck, it would be too humane for the likes of her.

"Why tell us all of this?" Crash asked. "Are you hoping we spare you?"

Dr. Fields wouldn't talk. For once, she kept her mouth shut. I tossed her to Kane and Crash. I had a feeling she'd started spilling her secrets to save herself from some torture.

"Make the bitch suffer, then find all her files on the three of us. Who knows what else she's been hiding."

I walked out, knowing they'd do as I'd said. Especially if it meant I wouldn't kill them for hurting Hollis. Little did they know I actually needed the two of them. It was better for them to remain clueless.

Chapter Thirteen

Hollis

My heart hammered in my chest, anticipation and dread warring within me. Riot had commanded that I wait for him here, and the thought of disobeying never crossed my mind.

"Welcome back," I whispered as the door creaked open, revealing his towering figure. His footsteps were heavy and purposeful. His eyes burned with sadistic intensity, promising pain and pleasure in equal measure.

"Miss me, did you?" he asked, slamming the door shut behind him. The sound ricocheted through the room, sealing my fate within his merciless grasp. I didn't know what happened while he was gone. He still seemed as angry as before.

Trembling, I lifted my gaze to meet his, where fear entangled with longing deep within me. "Yes."

"Good." He smirked, reaching out to stroke my cheek with his rough hand.

"Riot…" My voice was barely more than a breath, but he seemed to hear it just fine.

"Shh," he whispered, pressing a finger against my lips. "You don't have to say anything."

As much as I hated to admit it, there was something comforting about giving myself over to him completely. In a world filled with chaos and uncertainty, Riot was my one constant -- my anchor in the storm. Even when he inflicted pain, at least I knew he wouldn't go too far. Somewhere along the way, I'd learned to trust him.

"Just… don't hurt me too much," I said.

His laughter was low and dangerous, sending shivers down my spine. "Now, where would be the fun in that?"

The room seemed to shrink as Riot towered over me, his presence a suffocating force that left me gasping for air. I couldn't tear my eyes away from his piercing gaze, my entire being trembling under the weight of his stare.

"The doctor lied to me. Dr. Fields won't be with us anymore. Crash and Kane are taking care of her. She told me I was sterile. I'd thought there was no way you were pregnant with my baby. But now I know different. It's mine, Hollis, and so are you."

Panic threatened to consume me, my thoughts racing as I tried to process the horrifying reality of my situation. I was carrying the child of a monster -- bound to him in a way I could never have imagined. The terror that gripped me was unlike anything I had ever experienced, rendering me utterly helpless. Sure, being here on my own was one thing. But bringing a child into the mix? I couldn't begin to imagine it.

"Please," I choked out, tears stinging my eyes, "don't hurt our baby."

A cruel laugh escaped Riot's lips as he leaned in close, his breath hot on my face. "I'll keep it safe, Hollis" -- his words were a twisted promise, laced with sadistic glee --"but don't expect anything else from me."

I couldn't tear my gaze away from Riot's perverse smile, the malice in his eyes chilling me to the core. My heart pounded violently against my chest, as if trying to escape the prison that was now my life.

"Remember this well. I'll protect you and the little one, but don't think for a second that means I'll love either of you." He grabbed my chin, forcing me to meet his cold, merciless stare. "You're mine, Hollis. Body and soul. And the kid in your belly belongs to me too."

"Don't do this. Not to your own baby."

"Too late for pleading. You're both in my world and there's no way out."

My mind raced with panic, desperately searching for any shred of hope. But all I found was the suffocating darkness of my new reality -- trapped, bound to a monster who reveled in my fear. The weight of it threatened to crush me, filling my throat with bile and bile alone.

"Why are you doing this? I thought things were better between us. Did something happen?"

His grip tightened around my chin, causing pain to shoot through my jaw. "Because I can. You're mine, and I intend to keep you that way."

Left with no other choice, I clenched my fists and steeled my resolve. If I was to survive this nightmare, I would have to rely on my own strength and resourcefulness -- the very traits that had kept me alive in Raven's Vale thus far.

His dark gaze bore into me, and my mind raced with horrifying possibilities. As I stared into his cold eyes, I knew that fighting him would only bring more pain, more suffering. The only way to survive this nightmare was to submit to his abnormal desires, to play whatever sick game he had in store for me. Not only as a woman, but now as the mother of his child.

"Fine. I'll do whatever you want, just don't hurt the baby. No matter what you do, I won't let you destroy me." And I knew I'd have to do whatever I could to protect my child.

"Brave words. But we'll see how long that defiance lasts. Just remember there's nowhere you can run, nowhere you can hide from me. I own you, body and soul -- and I always will." Riot's dark eyes gleamed like a predator stalking its prey, an unsettling grin curving his lips. "There's something I haven't told you yet."

I swallowed hard, bracing myself for whatever new torment he had in store. My hands clenched into fists at my sides, nails digging into my palms. What new form of torture was he going to unleash on me now?

"See, I went to the trouble of implanting a little GPS tracker in your body. So even if you think about running, I'll always know exactly where to find you."

I could feel my heart plummeting into my stomach, the weight of my situation pressing down on me beneath its oppressive darkness. How could he do such a thing to me? My thoughts were a whirlwind of fear and desperation as I grappled with the reality of my new existence. Every time I thought I'd come to accept all the parts of Riot, he'd come up with something new that sent me reeling.

"I've only just begun, Hollis. You haven't even seen the depths of my darkness yet. But if it's any consolation, that little tracker is how I was able to find you before Crash and Kane could kill you. So think on that for a bit."

I knew my nightmare was far from over -- and that I would have to summon every ounce of strength and cunning I possessed if I wanted to outmaneuver this sadistic monster who now controlled my life. And the easiest way to set him at ease seemed to be through the use of my body. If I could entice him, then perhaps I could soothe the monster lurking inside him. Even though I hadn't fully healed, a bit of pain was better than Riot losing control.

I could feel the weight of Riot's gaze pulling me deeper into his twisted world. His eyes were like flames dancing across my skin, hungry for more than just my body. He wanted control over every aspect of who I was, down to the very core of my being.

His eyebrows rose as he stared at me. "I see the look in your eyes. Do you want me to fuck you?"

"And if I say yes?" I asked.

He chuckled darkly before leaning down once and capturing my lips in a searing kiss that left me breathless. His tongue danced with mine while one hand slowly drifted down toward my pussy which was already soaked through my underwear from anticipation alone.

He teased me mercilessly by running his fingers just along the edge of my panties without actually touching me where it hurt the most yet again displaying dominance over me, forcing a moan out of me despite myself as I squirmed under him wanting more... This time when his hand finally brushed against my clit it sent shockwaves through every inch of my body making lust take over any remaining semblance of rational thought.

The room spun around us as he took control both physically and mentally, pushing boundaries and breaking down walls. I heard the *rip* sound as he tore my panties and tossed them aside. Unbuckling his belt, he opened his jeans and pushed them down around his hips, pulling out his cock.

He gave it a lazy stroke and I watched as pre-cum beaded on the head. After pumping it a few more times, he dragged my ass to the edge of the mattress, bent my knees to my chest, and thrust deep inside me.

I cried out in surprise. There was a spike of pain with the pleasure as he roughly claimed me. Riot took me hard and deep, not seeming to care if I liked it or not. The feverish gleam in his eyes told me enough. I took each punishing stroke of his cock, closing my eyes and letting my emotions wash over me. Since he didn't know how to feel, I'd have to do it for the both of us.

"Look at me, Hollis," he demanded. I opened my eyes and held his gaze. He spread my knees apart and stared at where we were joined. "You look so pretty split wide around my cock."

Despite the pain and humiliation I felt from being used like this, there was something undeniably arousing about it all. The way he looked at me, possessive yet covetous at the same time, sent a jolt of electricity straight to my pussy. It was as though I existed only for him -- to satisfy his needs and desires however he saw fit.

It felt so wrong but also so right as he took control with each thrust claiming what was his. As he took me harder, I felt a wave of pleasure wash over me. He held my hips tightly, using them to control the depth and pace of his thrusts.

On the next stroke, I couldn't hold back any longer, and I came, crying out his name. The heat of his release filled me, and then he collapsed onto the bed beside me.

"You're fucking amazing," he murmured before kissing my shoulder.

His words sent a wave of heat spreading through me once again. It was clear that this wasn't just physical for him -- there was genuine emotion there too, even if he didn't realize it... it might not be quite what either of us were expecting when this relationship started, but that didn't make it any less seductive. Knowing I made him feel something was a heady experience.

"I'm upset about the tracker," I said. "But I'm glad you did it. If you hadn't, I'd probably have been tortured to death by Crash and Kane. Then you would have lost me and our baby."

He placed a hand over my belly and I covered his with mine. This was going to be the most fucked-up family ever, but it was ours. I'd been alone for so long, and now Riot had given me the one thing I always wanted.

"I didn't hurt you, did I?" he asked, lightly touching my wounds. The bruises had faded and were nearly gone. The stitches had come out, although the cuts hadn't fully healed.

"I'm fine, Riot. I needed that as much as you did. In case you missed it, I'm tougher than I look." I smiled at him faintly. "Although, I'd prefer not to put it to the test again."

"Come on. I'll wash you in the shower, then you need to sleep more. The doctor said you still need rest." He lifted me into his arms and carried me to the bathroom. Riot helped me remove my clothes, then took off his own. Once the shower spit out steamy water, he led me under the spray.

I'd never felt him touch me so gently as he washed my body and hair. I didn't dare bring attention to the fact he was treating me so well. If I did, it would probably set him off. In Riot's eyes, he was always cold and heartless. But he wasn't. Not really.

I didn't deny he was a killer, and remorselessly took countless lives. If it weren't for the fact any people who wandered into town and stayed too long were forced to remain here, the town would have died out long ago. I wasn't sure how it all worked, but I knew the sheriff and mayor had a system in place. I'd overheard them one day.

Riot, Crash, and Kane had no choice but to remain in Raven's Vale until the day they died. It was the only way to guarantee they wouldn't be locked back up. Which meant I was stuck here forever too. But I hoped one day, our baby would be able to venture out into the world. Unless they were a killer like Riot. And like me. He'd twisted and molded me until I became someone I didn't recognize. Then again, perhaps this was who I was always meant to be.

"You're thinking too hard," he said.

"Sorry. A lot has happened, and I guess I'm still processing everything. Especially the part about me being pregnant." I paused. "Did you tell Crash and Kane?"

He nodded. "They know, and they're aware if they ever try to hurt you again, I'll make them suffer. You'll be safe here now, Hollis. I promise."

I leaned into him, pressing my head against his chest. I could hear his heartbeat over the sound of the shower. It soothed me. I didn't think he'd like hearing me say as much so I kept it to myself.

"Tired?" he asked.

"Yeah. I think I need to sleep some more."

Riot shut off the water, helped me dry off, then carried me back to the bed. He rummaged in the dresser and pulled out a nightgown, helping me dress, before tucking me into bed. It was the most absurd thing ever. Never in my wildest dreams did I think I'd be tucked in by a serial killer.

"Sleep well, Hollis. I'll keep watch over you."

"Night, Riot," I murmured right before sleep pulled me under.

Chapter Fourteen

Hollis

The bed dipped under my weight, the springs groaning like they were sharing in my dread. I'd played this moment over and over in my head, each scenario more nightmarish than the last. Talking to Riot, The Butcher of Raven's Vale, about our child and my fears -- shit, it was like wrapping my neck with a noose.

"Spit it out, Hollis." Riot leaned against the wall, arms folded as he stared at me.

His shadow stretched across the floorboards, reaching for me like the fingers of death. I craned my neck to look up at him, feeling like prey cornered by a predator too used to the taste of blood. Actually, that was pretty accurate.

"Riot," I started, hating how my voice trembled, "we need to talk. It's important."

"Important?" He loomed closer, his eyes two shards of ice. "Last I checked, you don't decide what's important."

I swallowed the lump in my throat, hard as a damn gravestone. "Believe me, this is."

I sucked in a lungful of air, finding a shred of steel in my resolve. "Like the doctor said, I'm pregnant, Riot. And I'm scared shitless about how you'll deal with a baby who's crying."

His reaction was immediate -- a gut punch of raw fury. His face contorted into something dark and terrible. It was like looking death in the face. His hands curled into fists, knuckles bone-white.

"Shut up." The command was sharp and left no room for argument. But he stayed rooted, listening. There was an edge there, a razor-thin line between curiosity and contempt as he took in my shaking form. Maybe I could still make him listen, to understand. I knew it was risky. After all, he didn't know a thing about human emotions.

I sat there, trembling from the inside out, bracing myself against the storm I saw brewing in his eyes. His fists were tight, but his eyes -- narrowed into unforgiving slits -- were fixed on me like I was a puzzle he couldn't piece together.

"Riot, it's more than just the crying. It's... what if they end up like me? Bruised. Broken." I paused, trying to figure out how to say everything I needed to say without making him angry. "Your kid doesn't deserve to live in hell. I want to give them a better life than either of us had."

For a moment, the room felt so still I was scared to even breathe. The man before me, "The Butcher" of Raven's Vale, seemed to teeter on the edge of comprehension and chaos. A shiver crawled up my spine, knowing I was dancing with the devil.

"Say it again," he said, low and dangerous, yet there was something beneath the surface. Confusion? Uncertainty?

"Your child, Riot," I said, my voice hitching as I forced each word out. "I can't stand to see them suffer, not like I do, not under your rule. I want them to be happy."

His anger, the kind that fueled the nightmares of the entire town, flickered. Just for a second, it dimmed in his eyes, replaced by a shadow of something else. Maybe it was the thought of his own blood, vulnerable and innocent, that pierced the armor of his rage.

"Damnit, Hollis," he muttered, almost to himself. His ironclad posture slackened as he paced, the predator within wrestling with a foreign contemplation. "You think I don't know the risk?"

For a heartbeat, I saw it -- the glimpse of a man buried under the monster, struggling to break free. And in that fractured second, I dared to hope. It wouldn't be overnight. Possibly not even over several years, but bit by bit I thought Riot might be able to become more human.

I bit into my trembling lip, the taste of iron blooming against my tongue. "There's got to be a way."

As he continued to pace, I wondered what I could possibly do to keep our child safe. Then it hit me. I thought of Riot's room where he kept his journals stored. No one could go in there except him, or unless he let them in.

"A safe room," I muttered.

Riot halted mid-pace. He turned to me, and I wasn't sure what I saw in his eyes just then.

"Safe room?" he echoed, the words dripping with disdain, yet tinged with curiosity.

"Yeah," I pushed on, feeling the weight of his gaze. "A place... for the kid. If things get too wild, if you or your brothers lose it, there'd be somewhere to hide. Somewhere... untouchable."

Something shifted behind those eyes that had witnessed death more intimately than love. The harsh lines of Riot's face softened, as if my words had hit home, carving through the hardness of his exterior. A flicker of understanding sparked to life where only darkness had resided.

"Untouchable," he repeated, the word rolling off his tongue as if tasting a foreign concept. It wasn't tenderness that filled his voice, but rather a grim recognition of necessity. His head tilted slightly, the movement predatory yet oddly protective.

"Damnit, Hollis," Riot said, and for an instant, I could swear the beast of a man before me was weighing my life and the unborn's against his own twisted desires. "You think a room would keep the shadows at bay? Think four walls and a door would keep me or the others out if we really wanted in there?"

"Maybe not," I admitted. "But it might give us a fighting chance."

His silence left a chill in the room. But his eyes... they held a gleam that wasn't there before -- a reluctant admission that maybe, just maybe, I wasn't spewing nonsense.

"All right." It was the closest thing to consent I'd ever gotten from him. And hell, it felt like victory, even in this Godforsaken place. The simple fact he'd admitted our child might need protection from him, Crash, and Kane was a step in the right direction.

"Fine," he said. "We'll build your damn sanctuary. Not sure what good it will do, but I'll figure something out. Maybe a way to reinforce the door or something."

"Good." Relief flooded me, swift and overwhelming. The safe room would be a fortress within a fortress, a place where innocence might be shielded from the monstrous reality beyond its walls. I knew it wasn't perfect. Might not even work, but I had to at least try. I wanted our child to have something we never did -- a loving and safe environment.

"Remember, Hollis. I'm still in control. This changes nothing."

"Of course," I whispered. Except it really did change things and proved that Riot was slowly changing too. I didn't think he'd ever be a normal person. There was a part of him that would always need the kill, the hunt. He thrived on bloodshed, and there was no way to remove that piece of him. Not without losing all of him. But if I could just find the smallest hint of humanity in him, and grow it a little, then living here wouldn't be so bad. I might love him, but it didn't mean I wanted to risk the safety of our child.

I knew the notion of security was a cruel joke here, in the belly of the beast. But it was a joke I had to play along with, for the sake of the life growing inside me -- a life that deserved more than the shadows and screams that filled our twisted world. Their daddy might be a monster, a cold hard killer, but it didn't mean they couldn't be raised with love.

"Then it's settled. We fortify a room... for the brat." He shifted and folded his arms again, but I saw the vulnerability on his face. He'd felt something, and he didn't like it. Or maybe he just didn't understand it. Either way, it was a step in the right direction.

"Thank you." I watched him, this man, this monster, who could tear lives apart with his bare hands. And yet, in this single, rare moment, he had chosen to build rather than destroy.

"Save it. Just remember, no matter where you hide, I am always here. Even if you run into that room with our kid, you'll still have to come back out."

I nodded, silent, my mind racing with the logistics of our morbid nursery. The safe room was a concession, a small piece of ground gained in a war I was destined to lose. Yet, it was a victory nonetheless -- one I clung to amid the chaos.

"Get some rest," he ordered, without looking back. "You'll need it."

As his footsteps receded, the dread and hope within me waged their silent war. The safe room would be a haven, a sliver of light in the endless darkness that was life with Riot Tredway. It was a bitter pill, sweetened by the faintest hope that maybe, just maybe, survival was possible in this house of horrors.

* * *

Riot's hand clasped around mine, callused and commanding, as he tugged me from the bed several hours later. The softness had vanished, replaced by the iron grip of The Butcher, his name a whispered death sentence in Raven's Vale. We moved through the mansion, his steps thunderous, mine a hesitant scuttle beside him.

"Where?" His voice sounded more like the growl of a beast.

"Basement," I muttered. "Reinforced. Hidden."

Of course, there was the risk I wouldn't be able to get there in time. Something closer would have been better, but I wasn't sure it would be as safe.

He grunted, a nonverbal acknowledgment, as we descended the staircase. Each step felt like a descent into purgatory -- a place between salvation and damnation, where our baby could be spared or swallowed whole by Riot's darkness.

"Soundproof," I added. It would be necessary. A crying baby would possibly fuel their anger, and I might not be able to quiet the child.

"Smart." He snorted, almost amused, and I caught the briefest flicker of approval in his cold gaze. It was fleeting, but it was there.

"Cameras," I continued. "So you can see, make sure we're safe."

Once he'd calmed down, I knew he'd wonder about us locked away in that room. And this would give him a way of checking on us.

"Fine," he said in a clipped tone.

As we reached the bowels of the house, the air grew mustier, the shadows thicker. This would be the sanctuary for my unborn child, a macabre womb crafted by their father's twisted hands.

"Enough to keep the child out of harm's way?" I asked, my eyes scanning the dark corners, envisioning a crib amidst the gloom. Something would have to be done to brighten the place. And it certainly needed a good scrubbing.

"Out of theirs too." He glanced at my still flat belly. "Ours. I can't promise what will happen if I'm enraged enough. This was a good call, Hollis."

"Can't protect them from everything," I mused aloud, my mind a whirlwind of doubts. Would this small act of compromise be enough to shield our child from the depravity that lurked beyond these walls, within their own father?

"We can try," Riot replied, the closest thing to tenderness I'd ever heard from him. It was rough, frayed at the edges, but it bore the weight of a promise.

"Yes, we can try." In Riot's world, he'd never experienced a soft touch or known kindness. He had no idea how to love anyone. But this time, maybe -- just maybe -- he would be capable of building something instead of tearing it apart.

"Tomorrow. I'll have some materials delivered in the morning. We can start working on it then."

* * *

The chill of the unlit corridor seeped into my bones as Riot and I stood there, side by side. I felt his heat, a stark contrast to the cold that pressed in around us, and it was a twisted comfort. The very man who could end lives with his bare hands was now the shield between our child and a world hungry for blood.

"Ready for this?" he asked. "It won't be easy, and if I ask Crash and Kane for help, I can't promise they won't build in a way to access the room."

"Ready as I'll ever be," I muttered back, my heart hammering a frantic rhythm against my ribcage. I glanced up at him, catching the steely resolve in his gaze.

"Let's get to work, then," he said.

"Work" meant tearing down walls and building new ones -- fortifying a room where innocence could dwell, untouched by the chaos that reigned outside. A sanctuary amidst the storm of violence that was Riot's empire.

I watched his face, searching for a hint of the man beneath the monster. There was a hardness there that spoke of countless sins, but also… something else. A glimmer of understanding, maybe. It was enough to make me believe that, despite the blood on his hands, he could still carve out a space for something pure.

"Promise me," I whispered, the words slipping out like a prayer.

"Anything," he replied, his voice rough as gravel.

"Promise me they'll never know the horrors you inflict on those around you. That they'll think their daddy is just a tough guy with a big heart."

"Swear it on my life," he vowed, and I knew he meant every syllable. "At least, until they're old enough for someone else to tell them any different. I can only control this town to a certain point."

Our eyes locked, and in that moment, we were bound by more than the obsession and fear that had first bound us together. We were bound by a shared determination to protect the innocent life growing inside me -- a beacon of light in the all-encompassing dark. I had a feeling this child was going to change things. Not only for me, but for Riot as well. Possibly even for Crash and Kane.

None of them would ever be normal. I wouldn't ask it of them. But perhaps I could soften their edges a little.

"Then let's begin," I said, steeling myself for the path ahead. Standing there with Riot, the notorious psychopath with a merciless reputation, I somehow found the courage to face whatever came next. Together, we turned toward the future sanctuary, ready to forge a haven from the havoc, a safe room where love and madness could, against all odds, coexist.

It wouldn't be finished today or even tomorrow. It would take time, but together, I thought we might be capable of just about anything. This might seem like a small concession to most, but to me, I knew it was the biggest thing Riot had ever agreed to.

Chapter Fifteen

Hollis

I stumbled out into the choking darkness, the night air cold and biting against my skin. Raven's Vale was a ghost town, its streets barren and unforgiving. Anyone smart was tucked safely inside their homes. The echo of our footsteps bounced off the walls with a rhythm that matched my hammering heart. Riot moved like a shadow beside me, his towering form a constant reminder of the beast I'd shackled myself to.

"Keep up, Hollis," he said. "We don't have all night."

My breath came in short bursts, misting in the frigid air as I struggled to match his pace. Every instinct screamed at me to run, to hide, to protect the life growing inside me. But fear had become my bedfellow, and it compelled me forward, my hand splayed across my belly as if I could shield my unborn child from the sins of its parents.

The streets were like a coiled labyrinth perfect for the damned. We prowled through the darkness, hunters in a concrete jungle. The taste of bile stung the back of my throat, and I swallowed it down, along with the dread that threatened to overpower me.

"Scared?" Riot taunted, his lips curling into a smirk that never reached his dead eyes.

"Fuck you," I spat back, more to convince myself than to challenge him. My voice quivered, betraying the turmoil that churned within me.

"Careful now." He snickered. "Wouldn't want to upset the little monster you're incubating."

I winced, unable to deny the truth. What kind of life was I bringing this child into? A world where death was a lover, and darkness a cradle? I shivered, not from the cold, but from the realization that I was walking hand-in-hand with madness, and there was no turning back. Not to mention, there was always the chance my child would be born as a mirror image of his father.

We slinked deeper into the bowels of Raven's Vale. Riot moved with a predator's grace, muscles coiled and ready to strike. He paused for a moment, nostrils flaring as if he could smell the fear that clung to the night air like a second skin. I sometimes wondered if he really was human, or if the stuff of nightmares might be real.

"Ripe for the picking," he murmured, more to himself than me, his voice a low growl. His eyes flickered with a wicked gleam -- the kind that spelled out doom for whoever crossed our path.

"Where?" I asked, though I wasn't sure I wanted an answer.

"Shh," he commanded, a finger pressed to his lips. "Just watch."

A shudder ran down my spine, the thrill of the hunt igniting something primal within me, something I barely recognized but couldn't deny. Riot's presence was a drug, intoxicating and dangerous, and I was hooked.

There, in the shadow of an abandoned storefront, a figure materialized, lone and oblivious. A plaything delivered to us by the cruel hands of fate. Riot's arm shot out, halting me. With a tilt of his head, he beckoned, and my feet obeyed, creeping forward on autopilot.

The silhouette grew clearer -- a man, maybe, or a woman, it hardly mattered -- just another soul unlucky enough to cross our path. Riot's movements were silent, a whisper against the cobblestones, and I found myself mimicking him, every sense sharpened by the promise of what was to come.

"Stay close." He didn't look back to see if I complied. The command was unnecessary. Where else would I go? We were bound by blood, by darkness, by the twisted love that bloomed amidst the carnage we wrought together.

As we closed the gap, I could see Riot's fingers twitch, aching for the release only violence could bring. I watched, transfixed, as the demon within him stretched its wings, preparing to descend upon its next victim with unholy fervor.

We edged closer. The prey was just a shadow, a wisp of life in the darkness that called to Riot like a moth to flame. Each step tightened the coil in my chest, every breath laced with the metallic taste of anticipation.

"Almost there," I whispered. Raven's Vale seemed to hold its breath, and so did I.

I could feel the tension rolling off Riot in waves, a tangible force that made my blood sing. Our dance was silent, deadly -- a duet choreographed by the devil himself. It was wrong, all of it, but resisting had never been an option. Not when the thrill seeped deep into my bones, not when Riot's presence wound around me like a vise.

But then, I pressed a hand to my belly once more, a stark reminder of the life within, innocent and oblivious. My heart hammered, loud enough I worried Riot could hear it. What kind of mother was I, skulking in the shadows, craving the very darkness I should shield them from?

"Focus," Riot said beside me, the word a lash that snapped my attention back to the here and now. "Don't lose yourself."

I nodded, but his admonition echoed inside like a warning. Could I reconcile the monster I'd become with the mother I needed to be? Doubt crept in, cold and insidious, but I shoved it down. Now wasn't the time for weakness.

"Ready?" he asked, a smirk curving his lips, the moonlight glinting off the madness in his eyes.

"Always," I lied, the word a shard of ice on my tongue. We were predators closing in for the kill. And yet, with each step, the battle raged within -- desire versus duty, the need to protect battling the urge to destroy.

We were upon our prey now. My pulse pounded in my ears, a drumbeat of primal longing and dread. Tonight, at least one person would bleed and feed Riot's need, but at what cost?

* * *

Riot

The weapon felt alive in my grasp, its heft an extension of my own twisted soul. My fingers coiled around the handle. The night air hung heavy with bloodlust, a cloak that draped over us, suffocating and warm.

"I can't wait to feel it," I whispered, more to myself than to Hollis. My breath was a hot streak across the chill that had nothing to do with the weather. "The sweet give of skin, the rush of warmth..."

Having Hollis by my side made it even sweeter. I'd always thrilled in the hunt, and it never bothered me to be alone. But having her beside me, watching her kill, brought a smile to my face. It made me wonder if Crash and Kane were right and I was going a bit soft. At least, where Hollis was concerned.

I couldn't deny she made me feel things. Perhaps, this was as close to love as my depraved soul could ever get. I hoped it was enough for her because I had nothing else to give. I'd never offer her sweet words or warm embraces. It wasn't something I was capable of, something I couldn't understand.

All the men in town who bought their women flowers, showered them with jewelry, I'd always seen as weak. If I gave Hollis something, it would be an item she needed. Although soon, we'd need things for a baby.

The thought of my child growing in her womb made me pause. Just for a second. I had no way of knowing if our son or daughter would take after me or their mother. I'd agreed to let Hollis shield them as much as she could, but it might all be a moot point. If the darkness in my soul passed on to the life inside her, they would be every bit as bloodthirsty as me.

I wondered if Hollis could handle something like that. Knowing her own child was incapable of truly loving anyone, even their mother. I'd watch and wait, see how things played out. Until then, I'd do whatever I could to make her stronger. It was the only way she'd survive.

* * *

Hollis

My throat tightened at his words, my body tensely wired as I watched him. The way he had us hunting prey was vile and vital all at once. The contradiction of it clawed at my insides, even as my own darkness salivated for the climax.

Until Riot, I'd never thought myself capable of taking a life. All my years in Raven's Vale, not once had I ever hurt anyone. It still stung that I'd been chosen as a sacrifice. Maybe I'd been *too* nice. Not anymore.

"Let's do this," I muttered.

"Patience," he said, his whole frame coiled like a spring. "Wait another second. Almost…"

The person stepped farther from the shelter of the building, and that was apparently all Riot had been waiting for. "Now!"

It happened in a blink. Riot lunged, a beast uncaged, every muscle strung taut with lethal intent. His movement was a blur, a shadow unleashed from hell itself, barreling toward the lone figure ahead. His aggression poured forth, untamed and raw, a tempest of fury that knew no bounds.

I couldn't tear my eyes away, caught in the spectacle, the sheer force of his brutality. This was Riot in his element, a demon of destruction, reveling in the terror he invoked. And as his form collided with our prey, the world reduced to nothing but the savage symphony of his violence.

Blood sprayed in arcs as Riot's weapon found its mark again and again. I stood, frozen yet mesmerized, watching the man I couldn't help but be drawn to become the monster he was famed to be. His laughter, dark and twisted, cut through the night -- a soundtrack to the carnage he wrought with such sickening glee.

"Isn't it beautiful?" Riot asked, his voice a perverse caress as he turned his gaze toward me for just an instant, his eyes alight with a madness that both repulsed and captivated me.

"Riot…" was all I could muster, my words drowned out by another sickening crack, the unmistakable sound of bone shattering under his relentless assault. The victim's screams pierced the air, raw and terror-stricken. The noise was a living thing that clawed at my ears, demanding recognition, demanding empathy. But there was no room for mercy here, not in Raven's Vale, and certainly not at the side of a man like Riot.

"Sing for me," Riot commanded of the whimpering figure beneath him, his boot coming down with a crunch that snuffed out another cry before it could fully form. The violence grew to a crescendo, a brutal symphony with Riot as the conductor, wielding his weapon like a maestro's baton.

My breath hitched, each exhalation misting in the cold air, my heart pounding a frantic rhythm against my ribs. This was the world we were bringing our child into, a world where savagery was the currency of survival.

"Look at them, Hollis!" Riot bellowed, gesturing with bloodied hands to the broken body before us. "This is power! This is what we are!"

The night seemed to hold its breath, the only sounds now were the wet thuds of flesh yielding to force, of life being extinguished with every strike. And as much as I wanted to run, to flee from the horror, my feet remained planted, my soul ensnared by the grisly sight and by the man whose love was a dangerous, lethal thing.

"Riot, stop," I whispered, but it was lost to the wind, tossed aside like the discarded humanity we left in our wake. The darkness had taken over, and I, in my terror and awe, couldn't look away.

I watched, numb and transfixed, as Riot's frenzy carved a path of carnage. The darkness within him was a chasm so deep it threatened to swallow us both. His hands, those same hands that had caressed me with something akin to tenderness, were now instruments of ruthless destruction, painting the alleyway in shades of crimson.

"Can you feel it?" he asked, his voice barely human, thick with primal triumph. "This is our truth, Hollis. This is what we are."

My own breaths came in ragged gasps, mirroring the punctured wheezing of our victim. There was no denying the surge within me, an echo of Riot's own hunger -- a darkness I'd tried to bury, but now blossomed violently under his influence.

"Riot. Enough."

He didn't hear, or chose not to, lost in the glory of his savagery. My eyes, wide and unblinking, couldn't escape the magnetic pull of his actions. This was the man I loved, the father of my unborn child, a man as captivating as he was fearsome.

When at last the struggle ceased, and only the sound of our heavy breathing filled the void, I knew something fundamental had shifted. We stood there, covered in the remnants of a life he'd just extinguished, our shadows entwined on the cracked pavement.

"Look at us," Riot whispered, his voice softening as he turned to me, his eyes still alight with the embers of his insanity. "We're unstoppable, you and I. Together, we're gods of this damned place."

His hand reached for mine, and I didn't -- couldn't -- pull away. Our fingers slid together, slick with another's blood, sealing an unspoken covenant.

"Forever," I murmured, the word tasting like a sin on my lips, binding me to him more surely than any vow.

"Forever," he echoed, and in his grasp, I felt the terrible weight of our joined fates.

We walked away from the cooling body, the echo of its last breath still clawing at the silence. The night air reeked of iron and fear -- a twisted aphrodisiac.

Riot's grip on me was unyielding, his blood-drenched arms encircling my waist with a possessive ferocity.

"Look at you," he said, his voice a low rumble against the shell of my ear. "Beautiful and feral. I can feel your need, Hollis. You wanted to join me. Wanted to make him scream and beg."

I leaned back against him, the slick warmth of his chest seeping through my shirt. He was right. Some part of me had wanted to join him, to hurt that man. There was no denying it now. I was as lost in this madness as he was -- our souls stitched together with each thread of darkness we embraced.

"Monsters," I mumbled.

"Monsters," he agreed, his lips trailing a path of fire down my neck. "But we're alive, Hollis. More alive than any of those sheep pretending to sleep in their beds tonight. We see the truth. Only the strong can survive in this hellish place, and it's up to us to weed out the weak."

The raw truth of his words ignited something within me, a fierce joy that burned all the more brightly against the backdrop of his brutality. Riot's hands roamed over my body, and I reveled in the harsh touch. In this depraved dance, we were untouchable, bound by blood and violence.

I turned to face him, the remnants of his victim smeared across us both like war paint. His eyes burned into mine with a lust that matched the savagery of his soul.

Our lips crashed together. As I tasted the copper tang of blood, I surrendered to the havoc churning within me. The darkness coiled around us, a serpent constricting tighter with every pulse of our entwined hearts.

"Yours," he said between violent kisses, claiming

me as his equal in this grotesque realm he ruled. "If anyone can claim me, it's you, Hollis. Only you."

"Yours," I murmured. "I've never belonged to anyone but you, and I never will."

And there, amidst the shadows of Raven's Vale, we found solace in each other's arms, our love a twisted reflection of the monster Riot had always been, and the one I'd become.

Chapter Sixteen

Riot

I dragged Hollis through the streets of Raven's Vale, my fingers biting into her flesh. I'd likely leave bruises, yet another mark to show she's mine. The moon was a sickly sliver in the sky, casting just enough light to dance with shadows on the cracked pavement. Every building loomed as a silent witness to our midnight prowl.

"Riot." She yanked hard on my arm. I damn near stumbled, her sudden defiance a surprise I hadn't anticipated.

"What?" I asked, following the jab of her finger. There, cloaked in the ink of night, stood our next plaything -- a silhouette marinated in potential terror.

"Another kill," Hollis murmured. Her eyes sparkled, reflecting the hunger that gnawed at my gut -- a relentless beast that craved the scream, the chase, the kill.

"Looks ripe for the taking," I admitted, feeling the familiar pull of darkness coiling inside me, eager to strike.

My gaze sharpened, zeroing in on the shadowed figure like a hawk. But something was off -- the stance was too casual. The air around him seemed too calm. A liability. Something inside me twisted -- a warning. This one wasn't for us, not for our game. A gut instinct screamed at me to steer clear, but there was no easy way to make Hollis understand without spilling secrets that were best kept in the dark.

"Riot?" Hollis prodded, her voice tinged with impatience. I could feel her eagerness radiating off her like heat from hot coals, ready to ignite at the slightest whisper of violence.

"Change of plans," I muttered, my words clipped as I pulled her away with a force that brooked no argument. My hand clamped down on her arm, an unspoken command that we were moving on. The prey before us didn't fit the bill tonight.

"Hey!" Hollis snapped, her heels digging in as she tried to resist. "I thought --"

"Thought wrong." My tone left no room for debate. The dominance I wielded over her was as tangible as the blade I kept sheathed at my side. She was a wild thing, but even wild things bowed to the alpha's will.

Hollis glared up at me, fire and fury swirling in the depths of her eyes. But she followed, matching my brisk pace with reluctant steps. Each stride I took echoed with authority, a reminder of who ruled over Raven's Vale. And it sure as hell wasn't her.

The mansion loomed before us. A fortress of madness and luxury entwined, it squatted on the outskirts of Raven's Vale like a spider at the center of a web. I shoved open the front door.

"Home, sweet hell," I said, as Hollis trailed behind me, her presence a silent challenge to my authority. The air was thick with the scent of old blood and fresh anticipation.

Without pausing to savor the tension knotting the heavy atmosphere, I grasped Hollis' wrist and dragged her toward the grand staircase, the marble steps cold and silent beneath our boots.

"Riot, what now?" she asked.

"Time to clean up," was all I said.

We reached the master bathroom, a sanctuary of sorts where the horrors of the world could be washed away, if only for a moment.

"Strip," I commanded, watching with a

predatory grin as she complied. Her clothes fell to the floor.

I shed my own garments with mechanical precision, the fabric parting from my skin, revealing the ink and scars that mapped my history. The shower's glass doors shuddered open at my touch, and we stepped into the spray together. The water hit us hot and steady.

Her eyes closed as if in worship, the water tracing rivulets down her curves.

The hot steam enveloped us, a temporary veil separating us from the filth of our deeds. But even as the water sluiced over our bodies, it couldn't wash away the sins etched deep within our bones.

Steam fogged the air as I gripped her hips, pulling Hollis against me with a possessive snarl, my hands branding her skin.

"Riot," she gasped, her nails raking down my back, marking me as I marked her. Her pain was her pleasure -- and I reveled in every scratch she wanted to give me.

"Mine," I said, claiming her lips in a bruising kiss. My tongue traced the contours of her mouth, delving deep, tangling with hers in a sensual dance. I tasted the sweetness on her tongue and groaned against her lips.

"Do you like it when I call you 'mine'?" I asked, pulling back to look into her eyes. The answer was written all over her face -- she loved it.

"Yes," she whispered hoarsely. "I belong to you."

My cock throbbed against her belly, a heavy ache that demanded release. I wanted nothing more than to bury myself inside her tight pussy.

"Tell me what you want," I said. "Tell me how

bad you want my cock."

She swayed toward me, her breath hot on my neck. "I want you to fuck me hard. I want you to make me yours."

I pushed her against the wall, my fingers entwined in her hair. "You're mine already. Don't you ever forget it."

She nodded, her eyes wide with submission. I leaned in and captured her lips again, my tongue exploring her mouth. I nipped at her bottom lip, making her gasp.

"You like that, don't you?" I asked, my voice rough with desire. "You love it when I take what I want."

She nodded eagerly, arching into me. "Please, I need you to fuck me now."

I took her hand and led her out of the shower. Not bothering to dry either of us off, I took her over to the bed, my cock begging for release. I pushed her down onto the mattress and climbed on top of her, kissing her neck, her shoulders, her collarbone. She writhed beneath me, her nails raking my back again.

"Please," she begged. "Take me. Fuck me."

I groaned and positioned my cock at her entrance. She was so wet, so ready for me. I thrust into her, feeling her tightness squeeze around me. She moaned loudly, arching her back off the bed.

"Fuck! You feel so good."

I pounded into her, my hips slapping against hers in a rhythm that echoed through the room. She met every thrust with a moan, her nails clawing at my back, leaving trails of pain. I loved every second of it.

"You like that, huh?" I asked, my voice hoarse. "You like being claimed by me?"

"Yes." She whimpered. "Please, don't stop."

I picked up the pace, slamming into her harder and faster. She was all mine -- body and soul. As I felt the familiar tingle of an impending orgasm, I gripped her hips tighter and plunged deeper into her, claiming her completely.

"Mine," I gritted out. "You'll never belong to anyone else."

And with that, I released myself inside her, filling her with my cum. We collapsed together in a heap, panting heavily.

"You're perfect," I murmured, brushing a lock of hair from her face. "Absolutely perfect."

She smiled up at me, and I knew that somehow, I'd found the one woman meant to belong to me. She could be every bit as violent and as savage as me yet had a tender side that was a nice counter to my darkness.

I carried her back to the shower, and we quickly washed. "Need to get dressed."

"Okay," she murmured, hastening to obey. Once we were both presentable, I knew it was time.

"Let's go downstairs," I said. "There are things you need to know."

"About Raven's Vale?" she asked, eyes sharp and knowing.

"About everything," I replied, leading her out of the room.

I pulled my phone from my pocket, and quickly dialed the mayor. The beast in me was tired of skulking in the shadows -- it was time Hollis knew the depth of the darkness she'd willingly stepped into.

The moment the call connected, I barked out my orders. "Get your sorry ass to my mansion. Now. And bring the sheriff with you."

"Crash! Kane!" I yelled, my voice echoing

through the grand halls of the manor.

"Here," came a voice from the shadows, and the two figures emerged like wraiths. They knew better than to keep me waiting.

"Good," I said, my eyes flashing with a dangerous glint. "We've got a lesson to teach."

*** * ***

"Raven's Vale isn't run like other towns. You've already figured that much out. But now it's time for you to learn exactly how this place works."

Crash leaned against the wall, arms folded, an unreadable mask on his face that didn't fool me one bit. Kane fidgeted like a mutt needing to piss, but he kept his trap shut. The mayor and sheriff shifted uneasily.

"Scattered around this cesspit, there are eyes and ears -- my eyes and ears. They're the lifeblood of this place, keeping the chaos just shy of anarchy."

"Maintaining the population, enforcing the rules," Mayor Rawlins added, his voice barely above a whisper, the resignation etched deep within it.

"Exactly." I stalked closer to Hollis. "We've got our own brand of justice here. And there's shit we don't tolerate. No rapists. No other killers. That's our domain."

"Other criminals, though," Rawlins continued. "They roam free, some under Riot's wing. That shadow you pointed out, the one slinking in the alley? He's one of Riot's hounds. It's why you couldn't kill him."

"He sniffs out trouble before it festers. Reports back to me," I said. "There are a few like him lurking around. It keeps everyone else in line."

"So you knew who it was when I pointed them out?" she asked.

"I did and mentioned it to the sheriff and mayor before telling them to come here."

Hollis, her eyes wide but not fearful, nodded slowly. The veil lifted from her gaze, and she began to see the perverted tapestry of Raven's Vale, woven with threads of blood and terror.

"Understand now?" My voice was low. "This is my kingdom, our kingdom. And these are the rules you play by."

I watched her, the realization dawning, and something feral uncoiled within me -- a mixture of pride and possession. She was truly becoming part of my world, part of the very sinews that held Raven's Vale together.

"Beyond these streets," I said, "there's a world that doesn't give two shits about the poor bastards with no direction. But they're mine. They work for me. They breathe because I allow it."

I leaned forward, elbows on knees, hands clasped together as if in prayer -- though I'd never once believed in any god. "They scout the gutters, the dark corners of nowhere towns. Find the lost ones, the hopeless. Offer them a ticket to Raven's Vale. A second shot at life, or the closest thing to it."

My eyes flicked to Dalton and Rawlins. "The sheriff here, mayor too, they play good Samaritan. Jobs, roofs over their heads, all the things people want. Some bite the hand feeding them and end up on the streets again. Their choice. Our rules."

Hollis watched me. I could almost hear the cogs turning in her skull as she pieced together the grim mosaic of our world. Her eyes began to harden with the same resolve that coursed through my veins.

"Riot --" she started, but I held up a hand, cutting her off.

"Listen, Doll. This is the belly of the beast. You're in deep now. And there's no crawling back out. Not for you. Not for anyone."

I saw it then -- the shift. The moment her spirit snarled and snapped into place beside mine. She understood the game, the unspoken creed we lived and bled by. And she'd stay by my side, helping me keep the status quo.

"Got it?" I asked, gauging her, testing the mettle I already knew was there.

"Got it."

"Welcome home, Hollis." My lips twisted into something that might've passed for a smile in another life. "To Raven's Vale -- where the damned find their calling, and the wolves run free."

"But how does no one find out what's going on here?" she asked.

"Those who live outside and know of me and this place are loyal. Some of them I saved by killing the monsters hurting them. It wasn't intentional, but the end result was nice. They make sure no one speaks of this place, and no one comes searching for the three of us."

"And people willingly come here, even knowing they may die?" she asked.

"Hollis, people die all the time. If they stayed out there, living in the filth, then they would find their end soon enough. At least here, they have a chance."

She pressed her lips together in a tight line. "I didn't. I was born here, abandoned here, and never hurt anyone. So why was I chosen as a sacrifice?"

I grinned. "Because I asked them to choose you. From the moment I saw you, you caught my eye. Something about you called to me. It was the first time my initial reaction wasn't to slit someone's throat. Call me curious, but I decided I wanted to play with you a bit. See if I could figure out what made you special."

She paled a little and glared at me. "I'm not a toy, Riot. I know you often talk about me like I'm one, but I'm a living, breathing human."

I leaned closer to her. "Oh, but you are one, Hollis. You're *my* toy. If you've already forgotten, I can take you upstairs and remind you."

Her cheeks flushed, and she narrowed her eyes at me. I loved seeing that fire in her.

"Now you know how things work," Kane said. "And because of how we run things, your baby will always be safe here. Whether they're like you or Riot won't matter. There will be a spot for them in Raven's Vale."

Her shoulders sagged and she nodded. "All right. I get it. And thank you for explaining things to me."

"Did you say baby?" the mayor asked.

"Yes. Hollis is pregnant with my child." I stared at the two men. "Which means you are to protect her at all costs. Anyone says something rude to her, looks at her wrong, or so much as bumps into her, I want to know about it."

"Riot, I think that's going a little far," she said.

"I don't. You're mine. No one is allowed to hurt you except me."

She gave me a slight smile, and I noticed the exchange of glances between the sheriff and mayor. I hoped I wouldn't have to visit them individually and make sure they didn't cause trouble. It would be a hassle to put new people in their places, but I'd do it if necessary. And they damn well knew it.

"I understand, Riot. We'll make sure she's safe and comfortable," Sheriff Dalton said.

"Good. I'd hate for either of you to cause problems for me," I said, making sure they understood the underlying message. Both men nodded.

"Now get the hell out of my house," I said.

The mayor and sheriff left. Crash and Kane watched Hollis. I didn't see animosity in their eyes. Only questions. I knew there was a lot they didn't understand about my relationship with her. I didn't either for that matter.

"Did the two of you consider what I brought up before?" I asked. They both seemed confused. "About finding your own women?"

Crash shrugged. "I'm not actively looking. Maybe I'll run across someone who piques my interest like Hollis did with you."

"Same," Kane said. "Although, I like the idea of each of us starting families."

Hollis had a startled look on her face. "You do?"

Kane nodded. "The three of us can't live forever. We'll need to turn this town over to someone else one day. Might as well be our own flesh and blood."

Her jaw dropped open. "Are you saying you need heirs like a royal family or something?"

"Can't think of another reason to need a kid running around," Kane muttered. "Noisy pains in the ass, if you ask me."

"Do me a favor," Hollis said. "If you do approach someone, you might want to leave out the part where you intend to turn her into a broodmare."

Crash scratched his neck. "I don't know. Might make her fight more. Could be fun."

Hollis rolled her eyes. "I give up. The three of you really are psychos, you know that?"

I leaned in and nipped her ear. "Yes, but you seem rather fond of this particular psycho."

She smiled and kissed me. "Yes, I am. And I suppose the other two may grow on me. I'll just think of them as your pesky brothers. I've heard siblings can be quite annoying."

Crash reached for the gun tucked into his waistband and I shot him a hard look, freezing him in place. He slowly put his hand down. If he hadn't, I'd have beaten the hell out of him. However many times it took until he learned his lesson.

Hollis was off-limits to everyone but me.

Epilogue

Hollis
Four Months Later

I leaned back against the cold stone of the mansion's balcony, my gaze heavy with resignation. Raven's Vale, a place as twisted and dark as the man who ruled it -- Riot Tredway, The Butcher, my captor turned perverse protector. This Godforsaken town was a trap, but in its cruel embrace, I'd found a sanctuary for me and the life growing inside me. The irony wasn't lost on me. The safest haven for my child was under the wing of a psychopath.

"Safer with the devil you know," I muttered to myself, a bitter chuckle escaping my lips. Riot's reign was unchallenged, his brutality the only law we knew. And in this hellhole, his word was gospel. In the end, he had carved a place for me here, in the heart of darkness. It was a twisted affection, one that promised death to any who dared harm me or mine.

Violence was as common as the whispered prayers for salvation in this place. A scream in the night didn't summon help -- it only drew the curtains tighter across windows. If someone was lucky enough to survive the night, they didn't take chances by interfering in the matters of Riot, Crash, or Kane.

"Damned souls," I whispered as I watched a scuffle break out at the corner. Two men, both looking like they had more scars than untouched skin, were locked in a battle. Knives flashed, catching the faint glow from the flickering streetlamps. Blood spilled onto the ground, an offering to whatever gods still bothered to look upon Raven's Vale. No one intervened… intervention meant death, or worse, the ire of Riot.

"Survival of the foulest," I corrected my earlier thought, my hand subconsciously resting on the slight swell of my abdomen.

The air was thick with the stench of fear. The town was a beast, and Riot... Riot was its beating heart -- a heart devoid of mercy, save for the oddities of his twisted affections.

Here's where you belong, Hollis. The truth was a bitter pill, and in swallowing it, I secured a future for my unborn -- a future shrouded in shadow, yes, but alive. And in Raven's Vale, life was a precious commodity.

I made my way inside and into the nursery beside our bedroom. Once I'd made it through the first trimester and the doctor assured Riot everything should be fine, he'd let me choose a room. Aside from the safe room in the basement. The baby needed a place near us without being in the same room.

I leaned against the doorframe. Riot stood in the center of the room, his presence nearly overwhelming. He was constructing a crib, each movement methodical, deliberate -- a stark contrast to the chaos that was his usual signature. The wood groaned under his strength, but he handled each piece with a touch that was almost reverent.

"Damn," I muttered from the doorway, my eyes tracing the contours of his broad back, the way his muscles bunched and flexed under the strain of his task.

Watching him, this beast of a man who could snap necks as easily as twigs, fuss over dowels and screws -- it was a mind-fuck of epic proportions. And sexy as hell.

Riot didn't turn, but the air thrummed with his awareness of me. His hands, those weapons that had stained the earth red, now cradled the bars of the crib like they were made of glass instead of seasoned oak. The dissonance of it all -- his monstrous reputation versus this moment of almost sacred concentration -- sent a shiver down my spine.

"Always figured you'd build a gallows before a bed for a baby," I said, not sure whether the tightness in my chest was fear or something far more dangerous.

He grunted, the sound low and guttural. "Not an ordinary child," he said, without looking up. "It's mine."

Awe knotted with apprehension in my belly as I watched him, The Butcher, who could command the shadows and monsters of Raven's Vale, pouring his soul into a symbol of life amidst so much death. It was a contradiction that should've been impossible, yet there it was, unfolding before my eyes. In the last several months, I'd seen more and more glimpses of the man he might have been if not for his thirst for the kill.

"Careful, Riot," I whispered, half to myself, "you're showing your humanity."

His chuckle was dark, devoid of humor. "Nothing human about what I am, Hollis."

And he was right. Nothing human indeed. There was a chance any emotion I saw from him was merely him mimicking what he'd witnessed others do. Still, it was probably as close as he'd ever get, and I'd take what I could.

The echo of boots on hardwood floors pulled my gaze from Riot's tempting body. Kane was strutting toward me, a grin splitting his face that didn't quite reach the coldness in his eyes -- a predator playing at domestic bliss. In his hands he clutched a werewolf plushie, its fake fur matted and one eye hanging by a thread. Where the hell had he found that thing?

"Got something for the little terror," he said, thrusting the stuffed creature into my arms like it was some twisted offering.

"Figured it'd fit right in with the family."

The toy was grotesque, a caricature of the very beasts of nightmares. I couldn't help but let out a dry laugh -- this was what passed for a nursery gift in Raven's Vale. A fucking werewolf.

"Kane," I started, the words catching in my throat, "this is…"

"Perfect, isn't it?" His smirk widened, all teeth and no warmth.

I shook my head, not in disagreement but in disbelief. There was no escaping this place, no shielding a child from the savagery that seeped into every brick and bone of Raven's Vale. We were hemmed in by violence, born of it, and now, my child would grow up here amongst the three worst murderers within hundreds of miles.

"Thanks," I muttered. The plushie felt heavy in my hands, a symbol of resigned acceptance to the blood-soaked life that awaited us all.

"Every kiddo needs a beastie to cuddle," Kane said, oblivious or indifferent to the tremor in my voice.

"Especially here," Crash said, joining us.

"Especially here," I echoed, my heart leaden, knowing full well the kind of cuddling that went on under Riot's rule -- claws and fangs, screams echoing into the night. There was no sanctuary, only survival. And even that came with a steep price.

I turned the plushie over in my hands, its matted fur rough against my skin. I tried to remind myself it was the thought that counted, and Kane was trying. At least, I thought he was.

"A beastie for my baby," I murmured, trying to swallow the bitterness that threatened to spill from my lips. Kane watched me, his face split with that same self-satisfied grin that made my stomach churn.

"Damn right. Have to let them know from the start that Raven's Vale isn't some kind of fairy-tale land."

I nodded. The thing was hideous, but it was a gesture, something like kindness twisted into the shape of this town.

"I appreciate it, Kane," I said, forcing gratitude into my voice.

"Anytime, Hollis." He slapped my back, the sound echoing too loudly in the empty space around us.

The slap was still ringing in my ears when I heard the click of the last piece slotting into place. I heard footsteps walking off and knew I was alone with Riot again.

He stood up from where he'd been hunched over the crib, his large frame casting a shadow that swallowed the light. His hands -- those hands that had torn men apart without a second thought -- had assembled a sanctuary for the child that grew within me.

"Looks sturdy," I commented, the werewolf plushie now forgotten in my grip.

"Of course it is," Riot said, his voice low. "Everything I build, I build to last."

Why did I get the feeling he didn't mean the crib?

He stepped closer, and I could feel the heat rolling off him, the dangerous current that buzzed just beneath his skin.

"Even in this hellhole, I'll keep you both safe,"

Riot declared, his eyes burning into mine with a fierce intensity that promised violence to any who dared threaten us. It was the closest I'd ever get to a confession of love, and I was fine with it. Riot was who he was, and I'd never be able to change him. The little differences I'd seen during our time together would be all I'd get.

"Safe," I echoed, the word feeling alien on my tongue. Here, safety was as rare as innocence, yet somehow, in his presence, I believed it. Or maybe I just wanted to believe it, because the alternative was too grim to face.

"Nobody touches what's mine," he continued, the possessiveness in his tone wrapping around me like a barrier between me and the horrors outside.

"Nobody," I agreed softly, my resolve steeling within me. This was our life, our reality. And no matter how much blood stained the streets of Raven's Vale, we would stand together in the midst of it all, a twisted family bound by more than just fear.

I met Riot's gaze, searching the depths of his eyes for a trace of the man beneath the monster. There it was -- a flicker of something raw and unguarded, a vulnerability that belied his fearsome reputation. The sight sent a shiver down my spine, not of fear, but of recognition. I had found an unlikely home in his chaotic world, and I was as close to being in his heart as I'd ever get.

"Riot," I began, my voice barely above a whisper, "you're --"

"Complicated?" He cut me off with a wry smirk, the darkness swirling in his eyes. "Yeah, that's one way to put it."

The room seemed to shrink as he stepped toward me, a predator closing in on its prey. Yet I wasn't afraid -- not of him, not in this moment. His presence was both a threat and a sanctuary, a paradox that defined our existence here in Raven's Vale.

"Listen to me, Hollis," Riot said, each word laden with possessive force. "You and the kid -- you're mine. This town, these people, they'll never touch you. I'll see to that."

Even as I bristled at the thought of being owned, part of me relished the certainty of his protection. It was twisted, finding solace in the arms of a killer, yet there was nowhere else on earth where I could feel this perverse sense of belonging.

"Try to leave, and I'll hunt you down," he continued, the menace in his tone sending a thrill of danger through my veins. "There's no corner of this world where I won't find you, Hollis. Remember that."

"Is that a promise or a threat?" I asked, the challenge in my voice surprising even myself.

"Take it as you will," he replied, his words sharp. "But know this -- I don't make promises I can't keep."

As Riot's intensity enveloped me, I knew he spoke the truth. In this violent dance, we were partners 'til death did us part. And deep down, past the horror and the madness, I understood that I wouldn't have it any other way.

There was no escaping Riot's clutches -- not that I didn't crave the twisted sanctuary of his embrace. I watched him turn away, his back a wall of muscle and sinew, every inch the predator he was renowned to be. A dark yearning filled me.

"Fine," I muttered, mostly to myself. "We'll play house in this Godforsaken place."

He didn't respond, but I felt his approval radiating off him like heat from a blaze. My heart hammered a frantic rhythm.

Riot moved toward the crib, his hands tenderly adjusted the bars. His care was a stark contrast to the violence that seeped from the very air around him. The sight was surreal, like watching a wolf befriending a sparrow.

The crib, once just pieces of wood, now stood strong and sure -- a silent sentinel ready to guard our child. It was a symbol of permanence in a world where nothing seemed to last. And it anchored me to this moment, to the reality of being tethered to a man whose soul was a tempest of chaos.

"Will it hold?" I asked, my voice barely above a whisper.

"Like iron," Riot answered without looking up. His fingers traced the smooth edge of the crib, a gesture so delicate it was almost reverent.

I stepped closer, the floorboards creaking beneath my weight. The crib was beautifully crafted, and I fought the urge to reach out and touch the wood.

"Good." I let out a breath. I didn't just mean the crib. It was an acknowledgment of the life I had chosen -- or that had chosen me. The resolve hardened within me. I would protect my child with every fiber of my being, even if it meant living with the worst killers in town.

Riot placed a hand on the crib's rail, his gaze finding mine. Those eyes, dark as a raven's wing, held a glint that was both a warning and a vow.

I could see the outline of our lives taking shape, twisted and peculiar as it might be.

Perhaps we didn't have what most considered a fairy tale, or even a happily ever after, but for us, it was as close we could get.

As darkness claimed the room, it took with it any illusion of normalcy, leaving behind the raw truth of our existence. We were bound to survive -- no matter the cost. And I'd take whatever happiness I could find, even in the arms of a killer.

Harley Wylde

Harley Wylde is an accomplished author known for her captivating MC Romances. With an unwavering commitment to sensual storytelling, Wylde immerses her readers in an exciting world of fierce men and irresistible women. Her works exude passion, danger, and gritty realism, while still managing to end on a satisfying note each time.

When not crafting her tales, Wylde spends her time brainstorming new plotlines, indulging in a hot cup of Starbucks, or delving into a good book. She has a particular affinity for supernatural horror literature and movies. Visit Wylde's website to learn more about her works and upcoming events, and don't forget to sign up for her newsletter to receive exclusive discounts and other exciting perks.

Harley at Changeling: changelingpress.com/harley-wylde-a-196

Changeling Press LLC

Contemporary Action Adventure, Sci-Fi, Steampunk, Dark Fantasy, Urban Fantasy, Paranormal, and BDSM Romance available in e-book, audio, and print format at ChangelingPress.com -- MC Romance, Werewolves, Vampires, Dragons, Shapeshifters and Horror -- Tales from the edge of your imagination.

Where can I get Changeling Press Books?

Changeling Press e-books are available at ChangelingPress.com, Amazon, Apple Books, Barnes & Noble, Kobo, Smashwords, and other online retailers, including Everand Subscription and Kobo Subscription Services. Print books are available at Amazon, Barnes and Noble, and by ISBN special order through your local bookstores.

Changeling Press, LLC

ChangelingPress.com